Cross

A Gibson Boys Series Companion Novella

Adriana Locke

UMBRELLA
PUBLISHING INC.

Cover Design: Books and Moods

Cover Photography: Regina Wamba

Books by Adriana Locke

My Amazon Store
Signed Copies

Brewer Family Series

The Proposal | The Arrangement | The Invitation | The Merger | The Situation

Carmichael Family Series

Flirt | Fling | Fluke | Flaunt | Flame

Landry Family Series

Sway | Swing | Switch | Swear | Swink | Sweet

Landry Family Security Series

Pulse

Gibson Boys Series

Crank | Craft | Cross | Crave | Crazy

The Mason Family Series

Restraint | The Relationship Pact | Reputation | Reckless | Relentless | Resolution

The Marshall Family Series

More Than I Could | This Much Is True

The Exception Series

The Exception | The Perception

Note from the Author

Dear Reader,

First of all, thank you for picking up Cross.

I want to clarify a couple of things before you dig in. First, Cross is a novella. I wrote it initially for the Team Player Anthology in the winter of 2017. Since that anthology isn't for sale now and will never be again, I thought I would publish it on my own. **Please keep in mind that it was designed as a novella.** That means it isn't a full-length story with every detail fleshed out. It's a sweet, shorter tale of characters that I love and hope you enjoy.

Also, I've written a short story about Gibson Boy characters that was published on Free Romance Collections; it is no longer available on that site. Many of my readers have asked where to get it, and, because there isn't a place, I thought I would offer it in the back of this story. Therefore, you will get one short story after the conclusion of Cross. **Please expect this if you watch your completion percentage at the bottom of your device.**

I hope you enjoy Cross and Kallie.

Thank you for reading. I appreciate you!

Sincerely,

Adriana

Chapter 1

Cross

"Where have you been in that thing?" Machlan shouts. The roar of his muscle car's engine winds down and he clicks the transmission into park. The purplish-black paint shines in the early afternoon sun.

Having just backed out of a parking spot onto Main Street, I check my rearview mirror. No one is coming. "Bluebird Hill," I tell him. "After all that rain last night, I figured I'd test the new tires Walker put on my truck last week."

"You're a fuckin' kid." He laughs.

"Says the man driving that," I tease, pointing at his ride.

"I'm not sure what your point is. This car is the baddest thing in town." He punches the gas, the motor roaring like a banshee.

Glancing around at Doc Burns' office with two cars in the parking lot and the Linton County History Museum across the street that only opens for the Water Festival once a year, I grin. "That's not saying much."

"Go to Hell." His hand slips through his dark hair and over his chin. The amusement in his features evaporates as I watch ... and cringe.

I know this look. I know all of his looks, actually, a by-product of being his best friend as long as I can remember. Many of them concern me and a lot of them worry me. But this one? It's a flashing red sign with Vegas-inspired lights.

The thing is, I can't just ignore it. When this look comes, so does the topic of my sister and, even though I love the both of them, I wouldn't mind seeing them in a padded room until they fix whatever it is between them that is so broken.

With a sigh, I jam my truck into park too. "Yes," I say, answering the question he's yet to ask. "Hadley called and isn't coming home this weekend. She said maybe next week."

His jaw works back and forth as he stares down the street. "Why?"

That single word is spit with a lifetime of emotion. Machlan has loved my sister since the day she moved to Linton with our father and me when our mother died. She was fourteen and innocent and he was fifteen and infatuated. Through the years, they were off and on and together and not—at least officially. Everyone knew Machlan and Hadley were one and the same.

I'm not sure why she moved away from here. Being both *her* brother and *his* best friend precluded me from certain information, which is for the best. They both drive me nuts *without* having the details.

"Not sure," I reply. "She left a voicemail last night saying she wouldn't be home today. She didn't pick up when I called her back."

He flips his gaze to me. "You didn't talk to her after that?"

"She's a big girl, Mach," I mock. "I'm sure she had shit to do."

"Yeah." His fingers regrip the steering wheel as his jaw goes back to work again.

"I'm gonna go wash this before I head back to the gym—"

"She's all right, though. Right?" he interrupts. His face is stone-cold sober. "I mean ..."

"She's fine."

He waits. Blinks. Re-grips the wheel again. "That's it?"

Popping my truck into drive, I blow out a breath. "Yeah, that's it. You want to know more? Call her. What a fucking amazing concept."

"Yeah. I'll get right on that," he snips back.

"You should. Then you could quit this whole thing."

"Got nothin' to quit, man. Just being a decent guy."

A decent guy. It's my turn to turn my knuckles white on the steering wheel.

Machlan isn't a decent guy. He's a fucking great one ... much better than the guy Hadley is seeing now. A guy I haven't mentioned to Mach since I got home a couple of weeks ago from visiting her. I'm not mentioning him, either. I'll save the boyfriend an ER bill and myself the bail money.

I can't blame him. It has to be hard to see Hadley with another guy when, in Machlan's mind, she's his girl.

My stomach twists like it always does when my mind goes down this road. At least my girl didn't bring other guys back with her. Hell, she didn't even come back at all.

"Here comes Kip," Machlan says, bringing me out of my reverie. Nodding toward the road in front of him, he laughs. "I'm not moving."

I twist in my seat to see the sheriff coming toward us. He blares the siren twice as if to get us to move. We don't.

Machlan pokes his head out of the window. "Need somethin'?" he shouts.

Laughing, I watch Kip's car slide carefully between Machlan's and the curb on the other side.

"You can't park in the street!" Kip yells.

"What are ya gonna do about it?" I holler.

"Take ya both in."

"Don't you have somewhere to be?" Machlan asks. "Someone to protect and serve? Or *service,* if I know you?"

Kip shakes his head as Machlan flips him the bird. The sirens come on again before Kip hits the gas and speeds off down the street and vanishes over the hill.

When I look back at Machlan, his attention is on his phone.

"What?" I ask, curious about the smile on his face.

He looks at me and laughs. Sticking the phone in the cup holder, he shrugs. "Nothing. But can you do me a favor?"

"No."

"I need help moving a couple of things at Crave. Come help me. Just for a few."

"What's in it for me?" I ask.

"A beer?"

Throwing the truck in neutral, I rev the engine. It barely sounds before his is screaming over top of mine and we jet off in opposite directions. I get to a stop sign at the end of the street and do a quick one-eighty to head to Crave.

Chapter 2

Kallie

"Why are you smiling like that?"

Nora's question drifts through the warm summer breeze. Glancing over my shoulder, the amusement dancing on her face makes me laugh.

"What? A girl can't smile?" I ask.

"Absolutely she can, but can't her friend ask why?"

I try to shrug off her observation as I kick at a pebble lying on the sidewalk, watching it fall into the storm drain. "I don't know," I say. "Maybe it just feels good to be home."

We stop for a handful of cars along Beecher Street before we make our way onto Main. Nora takes out her phone when it chirps and whips out a few texts while I take in the town I grew up in.

Linton, Illinois is pretty much the same as it's always been. A traditional small, Midwestern town, the most noticeable changes over the last few years seem to be minor. There's a fresh coat of white paint on the post office and moss rose instead of impatiens filling the ever-present whiskey barrels lining the streets.

Closing my eyes, I breathe in the air, which is cinnamon-scented thanks to Carlson's Bakery and their famous coffee cake, a staple of my childhood. The scent brings back memories of summers with the windows down, Christmas caroling along Main Street in snow up to my knees, and the Water Festival in the fall that the entire town waits for all year. It's hard not to smile thinking about all that.

"I'm so glad you're back," Nora says, running a hand through her short blonde hair as we start across the street. My best friend since elementary school, she screamed when I showed up unannounced on her doorstep this morning. "When do you start work?"

"Next week. I'm starting over in the Merom office. Apparently, their attorneys have been sharing a paralegal and it's a mess." A hasty sigh sweeps past my lips. "I'm sure it's going to be a circus in there for a while."

"Yeah, but at least you're here. Linton hasn't been the same without you."

My laugh is light and free. "I bet."

"No, it true," she insists. "It's just me and the Gibson boys these days. Can you imagine how hard it is for me, the only girl, the only one trying to keep those boys in line?"

My smile falters, wobbling on my lips as I think about them. I have to look away from Nora.

"I mean, Molly McCarter tries to wiggle her way in there," Nora continues, scowling. "Every time I turn around, she has her claws bared and ready to dig into one of them. You should've seen her trying to land Machlan last weekend. It was disgusting."

"I forgot about Molly. What's she up to these days?" I haven't forgotten about Molly and I don't have one care in the world about what she's up to, but if I can shove off discussion about the Gibsons for a while, that's a win.

Nora snorts. "Besides whoring around? Nothing that I know of."

"What's she ever done to you?" I laugh, attempting to dissect her reaction. To hear her talk badly about anyone is strange, and there's a little more venom dripping from her words than I can just let go.

"Nothing. Nothing directly."

"Uh-huh," I tease, my curiosity more than a little piqued.

"Because that's a normal reaction for someone to have for a person who hasn't ever done anything to them."

She shoves her hands in her pockets, setting her gaze on some point in the distance, broadcasting pretty clearly that it's futile for me to press the issue.

We step across chalk artwork on the sidewalk outside the library and wave to Ruby, the seventy-something-year-old librarian who used to chastise me for bringing in Goldfish crackers during story hour when I was a kid. Her silver hair is pressed to her head by a pair of glasses, and a floral-print bag is draped off her narrow shoulders. I give her a little wave.

"Well, look who it is!" Ruby calls out, her frail little hand going back and forth in front of her. "Are you in town for a while, Kallie? It's so nice to see you, sweetheart."

I pause at the base of the steps leading up to the oversized doors of the library. "It's nice to see you too. How have you been?"

"I'm heading now to see Dr. Burns. I just have a little gout but he wants to run all these tests. The man doesn't have the sense God gave a goat." Ruby comes down to the sidewalk.

"Oh, Ruby." I giggle, helping her down the steps. Her hand clasps against my elbow as she steadies herself. "You should listen to him. He is a doctor, you know."

"Those fancy letters after his name don't mean he has any sense." She pats my hand and turns toward the parking lot. "Come by and see me, Kallie, and bring back that book you took out, Nora. The one about the...well, you know." She flits my friend a knowing look before unlocking her car door. "Kids these days."

"What are you checking out?" I ask Nora, curiosity piqued again.

"It's that one with grey in the title." Ruby shakes her head. "I had to order another copy because she hasn't brought it back in six weeks. Six weeks!"

"Just put my business out there, why don't you?" Nora laughs. As my laugh mixes with hers, Ruby shakes her head and climbs in her little maroon car. With a small motion of her hand as a goodbye, she pulls onto the street toward the only doctor's office in town.

"So, you love that book so much you can't bring it back?" I tease as we head down the sidewalk again. "You could've just bought your own copy instead of stealing from the library."

"Machlan has it." She sighs, rolling her eyes. "I took it to the bar one night when I figured we'd be slow and found him kicked back at a table reading it while I made drinks. He refuses to give it back to me. What am I supposed to do?"

"Machlan Gibson was reading *that*?" Eyes wide, I bite my bottom lip. The vision of one of the infamous Gibson boys—the too-hot-for-their-own-good guys I knew growing up—reading that book makes me shiver. "I don't think I can deal with that if he's even remotely as hot as he used to be."

Nora ponders this for a second. "You know how people age? Like wrinkles and beer bellies?"

"Unfortunately." Without thinking, my fingers pat at the crow's feet lining the corners of my eyes.

"Well, Machlan doesn't," she says easily. "I have no idea how he's still single with the women who throw themselves his way every night at Crave. I tell him one night I'm going to have to stage a diversion just so he can get home unscathed." Pausing to shoo away a dog yapping at the edge of a lawn, she turns to me again. "They've *all* aged well, Kallie."

I try to remain unaffected, to pretend like discussing our old group of friends is no big deal. It wouldn't be if we could stop with Machlan, Walker, and Lance Gibson and their cousins, Vincent and Peck, but we won't. It'll also include Cross Jacobs, and I'm not ready to do that quite yet.

"If Mach's still single, maybe you should hook up with him," I suggest. I know she'll shoot it down and she does—promptly.

"What?" she barks. "Are you kidding me?"

Laughing, I bump her with my shoulder. "It's not the craziest suggestion in the world. You've known him forever. He's freaking gorgeous. You like him."

"All of that's true, but I didn't say I was attracted to him." She makes a face like she's just bitten into a lemon. "He's like a brother to me now...sort of."

"Remember that time..." The sentence trails off as I catch myself, the rest of the words hiccupping in my throat. "Never mind."

"I know what you were going to say."

Peering up at her, I try to force the corners of my lips to turn up, but they refuse. "No, you don't."

"Yes, I do. When is the last time you talked to Cross?" The hesitation in Nora's tone only feeds the anxiety bubbling inside me, and hearing his name doesn't help either.

I've spent the last three years trying to forget Cross Jacobs. *Trying* is the operative word.

I don't have to ask if he still looks the same. I know the creases in his forehead that developed over the last year and a half like the back of my hand. I've watched through social media as he started to wear his inky black hair just a little longer than the buzz cut he used to sport, have noticed how he still gets it cut the first Monday of every month, like his father taught him to do. The playfulness I remember seeing in his jade-colored eyes has dimmed, replaced with something more stern. His shoulders are more broad, his body stockier than the man I used to curl up next to every night.

What I don't know these days is the sound of his voice at two in the morning or if he wears the same woodsy cologne, a scent that stops me in my tracks whenever I get close to someone wearing anything remotely similar. I wonder if he still favors basketball shorts to sleep in and who is there to time his boxing rounds like I used to do when he was training for a match.

My heart wrestles in my chest as I look at my friend, trying desperately to get myself in check. "When was the last time I talked to Cross?" I stop walking and glance up at the antique sign over our head that reads CRAVE. "The last time I stood here. That's the last time I talked to him."

I wait for Nora to push, but she doesn't. Instead, she tosses me a slight smile. "I need to run into the bar really quick and see if Machlan has my check ready. I don't work tonight and don't want to have to come all the way back to town later."

"Is it even open?" I ask, looking at the unlit open sign.

"It doesn't open for another two hours, but Machlan will be here. He practically lives here." The door swings free with a simple tug, the cool, salty bar air rushing out onto the sidewalk. "Come on. He'll be happy to see you."

Following her inside, my eyes adjust to the dim light. Alcohol ads glow from various positions on the walls, and strings of Christmas lights outline the mirror behind the bar and drape along a set of bulletin boards as I walk by.

All of that is hard to focus on with Machlan Gibson sitting at the bar. He leans back in the chair, dropping the remote for the television hanging in the corner onto the countertop with a flourish.

"Kallie Welch," he says, folding his arms over his chest as a smirk pulls at his lips. "What the hell are you doing here?"

"How are ya, Mach?" I grin.

He gets to his feet, a wide smile splitting his cheeks. "It's been a long time." Enveloping me in his arms, he gives me a warm hug. He's thicker, his back more muscled than the goodbye embrace he gave me before I left town in my little Honda Civic. "You home for long?"

"Yeah, actually," I say, pulling back. "The attorney I was working for in Indy got into some legal trouble of his own, and Mom's here alone now that Skylar moved to Wisconsin with her boyfriend."

"That explains why I haven't seen her around lately," he says. "Someone said she met a guy in Chicago, but you never know what to believe."

"She did. He's a nice guy. His family is from up there so Skylar moved up to be with him, which left Mom on her own, and I feel guilty about that."

"Because you're a good girl."

Nora clears her throat. "Now that's over with, you got my check ready?"

There's something Machlan wants to say as he processes Nora's question. He watches me carefully, like he's connecting some invisible dots scattered over my face. "Yeah, I got your check. Be right back."

He moves easily through the bar with such command that I imagine if people were standing in his way, they'd move. It's amazing to see him in this light. I knew he'd bought the bar, but seeing him as a legitimate business owner and not the immature party boy I knew before is almost unbelievable.

Turning toward the bulletin boards, I sigh. A warmth I haven't felt in so long causes the stress in my shoulders to melt away. Maybe it was the friendly hug from Mach, or maybe it's being back home in Linton.

"Want to get something to eat?" I ask Nora, scanning the boards.

"Sure. We could run to Peaches. They have great fajitas."

"It's still weird that a place called Peaches serves Mexican food," I say with a laugh. Running my finger across a set of papers advertising handymen services, I chuckle at one particular set of 'services' offered on a napkin. "This is ridiculous."

Nora laughs. "We take the really bad ones down—you should see some of them after a rowdy Friday night."

"I can only imagine."

"I can imagine a lot of things." The shock of the deep, husky voice behind me causes me to jump, but as the timbre of the tone settles, the familiarity washes across my heart.

I suck in a breath, capturing a gasp, though I'm not sure if it's is mine or Nora's. Inhaling the rich, almost velvety scent from behind me doesn't help the shakiness in my hands as I bring one to my throat.

One of my unknowns is answered: Cross wears the same cologne he used to.

Chapter 3

Cross

If Nora weren't standing beside her giving me that look, I'd swear to God I was seeing things.

The swallow I force down my throat is hot and heavy, as if it were laced with a shot of whiskey. It burns as it barrels its way to my stomach, but I don't register the drop into the pit of acid churning in my gut.

I can't do anything but stare at the back of Kallie Welch.

Her hair is pulled into a ponytail. I used to bury my face in the crook of her neck and kiss the top of her shoulder. She loved it. She loved me.

My stomach sinks as I take her in, fighting with myself not to reach for her. It's almost impossible to keep my hands to myself as I see the woman I think about every fucking day standing in front of me.

Nora looks my way before dropping her gaze and slinking to the side. The sound of her shoes against the floor as she makes her way to the back of the bar is barely heard over the white noise coursing through my veins.

I take a half-step back as I wait for her to turn around. She sighs, lets her hand fall to her sides, but doesn't move.

"What are you doing here?" My voice is rougher than I intended.

"Nora is picking up her check." Her voice is just a whisper, quieter than I expected.

"That's not what I mean."

She brings a hand up to the side of her face, the simple diamond stud in her ear catching a ray of sun streaming through the windows. As my lungs fill with air and refuse to let it go, I drag my gaze down her slender neck, over her dainty shoulders, and down her arm until it rests on her left hand.

My jaw sets, my teeth grinding so hard I can nearly hear the squeal of enamel scraping against itself. It takes everything I have not to lurch forward and jerk her hand toward me so I can see if she's sporting a wedding band. She keeps it angled so I can't see it; whether it's on purpose or not doesn't matter. Whether it's ridiculous of me to get pissed about something like that doesn't matter either. Just when I'm ready to pounce, she moves her wrist just enough so I can see her finger is bare.

"I, um, I'm moving back—I *moved* back," she corrects, nodding her head once.

I don't say another word. I don't move a muscle. I just stand in place and listen to my heart beat so hard, like it's chanting her name so she'll turn around and look at me.

Her shoulders pull back as she pivots, turning her body so she's facing me. *Finally*.

Remaining impassive is impossible as I take in the girl I once thought I'd marry. She's more beautiful than ever with her porcelain skin, full lips, and intense brown eyes. I look ridiculous standing in front of her, not saying a word, but all I can do is fight every instinct shuffling inside me.

"How are you?" I finally ask, shoving my hands in my pockets as a security measure.

"Good. Fancy seeing you here, of all places." She flinches as she says the words, a throwback to the fight that finally ended things between us for good. She takes a step toward me, her eyes wide. "I didn't mean it like that."

"Yeah, you did."

"Cross..."

Her eyes flood with a mix of emotions swirling so hard I can't separate them out. I could do what people do—pick out the one I want to see and roll with it—but I'm not most people, and I'm not a pussy.

"You look good, Cross," she whispers, quieter this time, studying me.

"You haven't changed a bit."

She shakes her head, running those ring-free fingers through her hair. "That's a nice thing to say. Total lie, but nice, anyway." She laughs.

"Why is that a lie?"

"Look at me."

"From where I'm standing, time couldn't have been any sweeter to you, Kallie girl." A smile tickles my lips as her cheeks flush. This is the girl I remember and, if I'm not careful, the one I'll once again be jacked up over in a heartbeat.

"Look at you being all charming."

"It's a new trick I picked up while you were gone. I figured I needed to round out my game a little."

"How's that working out for you?" She tries to play her question off like it's routine banter, but I know her too well. She's digging, prying, asking what I've been up to without having to ask.

"Win some, lose some," I say, looking her in the eye. Rocking back on my heel, I narrow my eyes. "What do you think?"

"About what?"

"Am I winning or losing right now?" My mouth fights the twitch of a smile crawling up my lips.

She takes a deep breath, steadying herself. "I'd say if we're taking into consideration the previous rounds, it's a split decision. This round doesn't look bad, but the ones before it weren't too pretty."

Trying to hide my amusement at this girl using, of all things, a boxing metaphor on me to describe our relationship, I shrug. "I don't think *all* the previous rounds were bad. I distinctly remember winning a couple of them. Hell, I thought I had the thing won a couple of rounds ago."

"You almost did," she says carefully, her voice steady now. "But that slip in the last round cost you the whole fight."

"I didn't slip," I insist, taking a step toward her. "I had a bad game plan."

"I can only score it as I see it."

There's a blip of pain in her eyes as her uncertainty fails to mask the wavering in her voice. The sound batters my heart, just like it did when she and I were together and I'd see a similar look on her face. I hate it.

We stand in the middle of Crave and don't say a word. The only sound is the shaky breaths escaping her sweet, full lips. A part of me wants to fight with her, tell her how stupid she was for walking out of my life and destroying everything I had planned for our future. Another part of me wants to toss her to the floor and fuck her so deeply, so completely that she remembers the connection and chemistry only we have together. Yet, there's another piece of me that wants to grab her and wrap my arms around her waist and hold her close if for nothing but to make sure she's all right.

"You said it's a split decision," I say, standing so close to her, our chests are almost touching. She smells of vanilla and the shampoo she always uses, the one in the red bottle. I fill my lungs with the scent of her and blow it out slowly. "Does that mean there's still a fight?"

She tucks another strand of hair behind her ear. "The bell rang on this fight a long time ago, Cross."

"Maybe the scorekeeper was wrong."

"Maybe—" She's cut off by the sound of Nora and Machlan

behind me. She looks at the floor and takes a step back, like we've been caught doing something we shouldn't.

Looking over my shoulder, I shoot a glare at my best friend. "What's up, Machlan?"

"I hate to bother you two, but I gotta get this place ready to open. You can use my office, if you want."

"I think we're ready to go," Kallie says, peering around me. "You ready, Nora?"

"If you are."

"Kallie, wait." There's no denying the eagerness in my voice, but I'm too focused on not letting her out of here without some sort of commitment to worry about it.

She keeps her sights set on Nora. "What, Cross?"

"What are you doing tonight?" I ask. "Or tomorrow night?" My mind races through my calendar, trying to figure out on the fly how I'll rearrange my appointments if she takes me up on one of my offers.

"I'm pretty busy…"

"Oh, you are not." Machlan smirks, leaning against the bar.

"Stay out of this," she says, flashing him a look. "This has nothing to do with you, Mach."

"Everything that happens inside my bar has something to do with me," he teases. "So, let's cut the shit: you really have nothing to do but you're still pissed off about something that happened years ago. Sound about right?"

"Enough," I say, firing a warning shot at him.

He laughs. "Fine. Just thought I'd help you two get to the point. See you tomorrow, Nora?"

"Yup," she says before looking between Kallie and me. "I'll be outside."

My eyes lock with Kallie's as the door latches behind Nora. "Name the place and time and I'll make it happen."

"Make what happen?" She sighs.

"Coffee. Dinner. A fucking slice of watermelon from Dave's Farmstand, if that's what you want," I joke…kind of.

"Is that still open?" Her eyes sparkle, the easygoing Kallie I remember starting to come back. "How many watermelons did we eat from there over the years?"

"I think the two of us kept him busy."

"Do you remember when Peck tried to make his own watermelon moonshine?" She laughs. "He was sick for a week, and then you all were trying to find a nurse to check him out so you didn't have to tell his mom."

"I forgot about that." I chuckle. "He was sick as hell. Lance finally found a nurse somewhere."

"Leave it to Lance." She giggles, wiping a tear from her eye.

"We loaded Peck in the back of Walker's truck and met her at the Four-Way Bridge to get checked out. What a mess that was."

"Does Walker still have Daisy?" she asks, alluding to the big black pickup Walker has driven since his senior year of high school.

"I think Walker will drive Daisy until he dies. He loves that truck," I say, shaking my head. "But back to the watermelon—Dave closed it down a while back. His wife got put in a nursing home and she passed away not too long ago."

Kallie's face falls. "She was so sweet. That makes me sad."

"I see Dave sometimes over at Crank," I say, referring to Walker's car repair shop. "Ran into him at Goodman's gas station a couple of days ago too. He asked about you."

"Why would people ask you about me now?" She considers this for a long moment. "Doesn't that seem strange?"

"Maybe it seems perfectly normal." Unable to resist any longer, I cut the distance between us in half. With a calculated move, I raise a hand and touch the side of her face. She sucks in a breath, her skin warm and smooth under my calloused palm. "This seems perfectly normal too."

"Cross..." She pulls her cheek away, her chin dipping to her chest. "I can't with this."

"You're right," I say, stepping back. Her gaze shoots to mine, surprised etched on her pretty features. "This isn't the place. Meet me at the gym tonight at six. We'll grab something to eat and take a ride or go for a walk or sit on the mats and shoot the shit."

Before she can decline, I head for the door.

"Cross! I didn't say—"

The door shutting behind me as I walk outside cuts off the end of her sentence. Nora is waiting.

"Kallie giving you a hard time?" she laughs.

"Never." I chuckle, shaking my head.

"I think she's a little shocked."

"One question," I say, turning around and walking backward toward my truck, the sun warming my face. "Did you know I was here?"

"Well, I knew Machlan wouldn't have my check until Monday, and I also know you drive the silver Dodge Ram parked right over there, so you figure out what I did and didn't know."

A laugh I haven't felt slip by my lips so easily in years bellows out. "Nora, I owe you one."

"Yes, you do."

Chapter 4

Kallie

"Do you still want to go to Peaches?" Nora asks. There's a forced easiness to her tone, like we just didn't walk all the way to the car and drive almost the entire way to my mother's house in silence.

"No."

Every step we took from the bar had me wanting to look over my shoulder in hopes of catching a glimpse of Cross. Every mile we pull away has me wanting to yell at Nora to turn around.

My head spins with the offer to see him again. My cheek sings with the memory of his touch. My heart aches as it absorbs the instructions from my brain to not forget the bad in favor of the good.

The endless partying with Machlan. The gossip. The rumors of wild nights without me in tow.

The two times I had to bail him out of jail for reckless driving and disorderly conduct.

His failure to take anything seriously or make a plan for the future.

A chill rips through me despite the warm summer sun.

"I really wanted a margarita," Nora says, turning toward my mother's house. "Are you sure you don't want to go to Peaches?"

"I'm not hungry."

"You're not hungry or you're mad at me? I'm really feeling like 'I'm not hungry' is a passive-aggressive and untrue response."

"I'm not mad at you," I say finally, watching the bright green grass roll by. "Although I know that was a setup."

"Maybe, maybe not."

"Don't lie to me." I laugh. "You totally set that up."

"What can it hurt?" She sighs, turning into the driveway. "I know it's none of my business, but…"

Her forehead is creased and her knuckles re-grip the steering wheel. Settling into the soft leather seat, I lean my head against the headrest. The adrenaline recedes, leaving me with a sluggish, almost hangover-style feeling in place of the excitement from a few minutes ago.

"He always asks about you," she says softly. "I never told you that because it felt like it didn't matter, but he does. Every time I see him, he says hello and then his features fall a little bit and he asks how you're doing." She glances at me over her shoulder. "He's not a bad guy, Kallie."

"He never was." The words land on my own ears and my spirits fall. "He's just not a guy that equals forever for me. Too much bull-shit with that one, no matter how much I want to pretend it's not true. I walked away once for a reason."

"Maybe he's not the guy you remember."

"Leopards don't change their spots, Nora," I say, unbuckling my seat belt and grabbing my purse. "Thanks for the ride."

"Call me tomorrow. Let's do lunch or something." She touches my shoulder. "I'm so glad you're back."

"Me too. Talk to you tomorrow."

Climbing out of the car, I shut the door. Nora honks the horn twice before pulling onto the street.

My mom's home sits in front of me, a little white square with dark green windows. There's a carport on one side that offers little protection from the wind in the winter, and my stomach twists that I've not been able to get it replaced yet.

"Someday," I mutter as I climb the stairs to the front door. It opens before I get to the top. "Hey, Mom."

"I thought I heard a car out here. I'm not used to having visitors." She smiles, letting me by. "Did you have fun with Nora, honey?"

"Yeah. We walked around town, and I talked to Ruby at the library. I can't believe she's still alive."

"Kallie Rae!" She laughs as she follows me to the kitchen. Pictures of me from various ages line the walls of the hallway. "See anyone else?"

"Machlan."

"How is he?" she presses.

"Good."

Pulling out a chair, she drops into the seat. "I saw him a few weeks ago at the post office. Good-looking boy."

"He's all right," I say, shaking my head.

"All right? Sometimes I'm not sure you're my child." She chuckles. "If I were your age, I'd have snapped up one of those Gibson boys in a heartbeat."

Turning away, I look out the window over the sink. The small back yard is tidy, her trash and recycling cans in a neat line by the gate. My old brown swing set still sits by the fence in the back, and the picnic table where I had dozens of chats with my friends growing up is in need of a good dose of paint.

All of these things are better topics than dating, or Machlan, or the one I know is coming: Cross.

My mother loved him like he was her son. She made sure he had homemade macaroni and cheese when he was over for dinner and always had his favorite soda in the fridge. When we broke up, she supported me, but I know down deep, she wishes things had worked out.

Maybe I wish that too.

Maybe wishes are pointless.

"We could get some paint tomorrow and redo the picnic table," I say.

"I wouldn't be able to move for a week."

The room gets quiet. The quieter it gets, the louder I hear my heartbeat.

"I'm supposed to go to my women's club meeting this evening with Dina. Do you want to go?" she asks. "Or did you make plans with Nora?"

Glancing at the clock, I see I have an hour until Cross asked me to meet him. My chest rises and falls, my fingers tapping on the counter.

"Well, you're invited if you want to come." She groans, getting out of the chair. "I'm leaving in about an hour. Let me know if you want to join, honey."

Her steps get softer as she pads down the hallway, and I'm left standing in the kitchen with nothing but a decision to be made.

———

Slipping on a pair of cotton shorts and a tank top after my shower, I make my way into the living room. The hardwood floor creaks as I traverse the room and plop unceremoniously onto the plaid sofa. The remote is on the other side of the room and I don't have the energy to get it. Besides, the quiet is something I kind of love.

Living in the city made me forget what silence really is. There are no tires squealing or sirens blaring, just an occasional dog barking from the house across the street.

The room is filled with mementos of my life that could only be collected by a mother. A frame hangs to the right with every school picture I ever took. An art piece I created in fifth grade is propped up on a bookshelf, and a trinket we bought on a vacation at Lake Michigan sits next to the television. Each one of those things has a memory of Cross tied to it.

My heart sinks as I squirm on the sofa. There's a hole in my chest that seems to have reopened since I pulled back into Linton, a big, gaping crevice that I was able to fill well enough in Indiana with work and hobbies and remembering things how I chose to remember them, but now? It's not that easy.

I had to force myself to get into the bath and shave my legs so I wouldn't run to the gym to see him on a whim. I washed my hair twice and then used a conditioning mask just to kill time. By the time I got out, I knew he would be gone.

A low rumble from the other side of the wall sounds through the air. Swinging my legs to the floor, I sit up and listen. It trails to the front of the house and stops. There's a long pause, then a squeak, and then it starts again. Jumping up and heading to the front window, I peer out of the curtains.

My breathing halts, my hands shaking as they hold the lace fabric out of the way.

Cross is dragging my mother's trash can from the back of the house to the street. He lines it up next to another one and brushes his hands off. Without looking up at me, he disappears into the back yard again.

"What the hell?" I whisper, dropping the curtain.

Finding my sandals, I slip them on and scurry to the kitchen door. When I step into the yard, he's latching a cable through the handles on the doors of the shed in the back corner.

Wearing a pair of grey jogging pants and a red t-shirt, he looks tall and lean and as broad as the shed. A darkened spot between his shoulder blades flexes and pulls as he works the cable. The fabric pulls tight along his muscles, giving me an idea of their definition and making my knees weak.

He turns around abruptly, catching us both off guard.

"Hey," he says, stopping in his tracks.

"What are you doing here?"

There's a smile that flashes briefly, but it doesn't give me the warm fuzzies. "I'm not here to bother you, if that's what you're thinking."

"Cross..." A lump takes root in my throat as I step across the soft grass. Sitting on top of the picnic table, I look at him still standing by the shed, just a few feet away.

So many summers we hung out back here in a swimming pool that's since been removed. We played badminton when I went through an obsessive stage with that game and watched the fireworks from a big trampoline we sold in a yard sale the summer before I left.

Our first kiss took place back here under the oak tree, and we buried Fluffy, my poodle, together near the back fence.

All of this hits me like a flood as my gaze locks with his, and when he speaks, the tone of his voice makes me think maybe it hit him too.

"I take your mom's trash to the road every week. While I'm here, I do some odds and ends I see she needs done. It's not a big deal," he says softly.

My heart slams against my ribcage, knocking the wind out of me. "You do? Since when?"

"I've done this for a long time, Kallie. It's no big deal."

"But...why? Why would you do this?"

His shoulders rise and fall. He rocks back on his heels, twisting his lips together. "What does it matter?"

"I had no idea," I say, forcing a swallow.

"I asked her not to tell you." He heads toward the gate, taking a curved path so he doesn't get too close to me.

"Cross, wait," I say, jumping off the table. The words are out of my mouth before I even know I've said them, and I have no idea what to follow them up with. There are so many things in my brain competing for a chance to roll off my tongue, and I know I better weigh them all carefully before I choose a thought I don't want shared.

He turns to face me, his brows lifted toward the sky. "What?"

Sucking in a breath, I plead with my brain to use the right filter and go for it. "Thank you."

He averts his jade eyes, settling his gaze somewhere in the distance. I take the opportunity to study him without the usual glare of a computer screen.

His jawline is more defined, the angle visible even under the day-old scruff. His lashes are thicker and darker, outlining the set of eyes that seem to have seen so much and, when they turn back to find mine, it causes me to jump. He tries not to notice, but his sly smile gives it away.

"Sorry," I grumble, fiddling with a strand of hair.

"Let's flip the script for a minute and you tell me why you moved back to Linton."

Clearing my throat, I pause. "Well, my old boss seems to be heading to jail for a while. Skylar moved away so Mom was alone, and it's easier to start again here than in Indy."

He doesn't blink.

"What?" I ask, furrowing a brow at his lack of a reaction.

"Just waiting for you to tell the truth."

"Um, I did." On instinct, I tilt my head at him, annoyed.

"Uh, ya didn't."

"Whatever," I huff, walking away from him. I stop at the fence and look over the top at the setting sun, feeling a little peace fall over me. The sky is painted a beautiful mosaic of pinks and purples, like a painting done by a master artist. "It's beautiful, isn't it?"

His hand touches the small of my back as he steps beside me. Suddenly, the sky isn't on my radar anymore. All I can focus on is how his hand feels on me, how every nerve is acutely aware of his presence and the pull of his body on mine.

"It is beautiful out here tonight," he says softly, "and the sky is pretty too."

My cheeks flush as I look at him. "You really can turn on that charm, huh?"

"I don't try it too often, but I'm hoping it works out for me today."

"Why are you helping my mom, Cross?"

"Well, the way I see it," he says, leaning on the rail, "she took care of me for a lot of years when I needed it. She hemmed my baseball pants, went to bat for me when Mr. Varian suspended me my junior year...and how many nights did she have something hot and ready for me to eat after practice?"

"A lot." I smile. "How many times did she make corn because you liked it and not green beans because you didn't? I hated you because green beans are my favorite."

We exchange a laugh that's easy and carefree, like two friends on a level most people never ascend to. Once our voices have died down, he pulls away and looks me in the eye. "For the record, I've never hated you. Not even when you left here with half of my heart."

I don't know what to say to that, but even if I did, it wouldn't matter. The searing gaze penetrating mine halts any words from flowing through my lips.

"I want you to know that." His head dips, his sneaker running back and forth across the lawn. "I take responsibility for everything that happened between us."

"Cross—"

"No, it's my fault. I was the shithead who couldn't get my life together." He raises his eyes, a glimmer in the jade orbs. "I admire you."

"Me?" I snort. "Why?"

"You were smart enough to know your worth." He lays a hand over mine, his palm hot and heavy and swamping mine in size. I can't look away from them, his tanned skin sitting atop mine. "You taught me a lot, made me who I am, in a roundabout, heartbreaking kind of way." He chuckles.

"Aren't you full of surprises?" I ask, his words wrapping around my chest and squeezing it so tight I can barely breathe.

"There's a lot you don't know about me."

There's a niggle in my stomach, something rooted terribly deep, that tells me he's being honest.

"Strangely, I believe that," I admit.

He twists around and leans against the fence. "Good. I'm an open book, you know. Want to talk? Ask questions? Kiss me?"

"No." I laugh, taking a step back for my own good. "I just got out of a job that had federal investigators asking me a million questions, and then I packed up my things and moved home. I don't need any more complications for a minute."

"Maybe I won't complicate it." He shoots me a grin that melts me from the inside out.

Pointing a finger his way, I giggle. "You always do."

"How's that?"

"That grin—it complicates everything, every time."

It stretches across his face, reaching from ear to ear, and it pulls mine right along with it. We stand in the setting sun, grinning at each other like two kids as my mother wanders into the back yard.

"What are you kids doing out here?"

My entire body sags at the interruption as Cross snickers.

"Just taking the garbage to the road, Brenda."

"Looks to me like you were doing more than that, Mr. Jacobs."

"Oh, Mom, hush."

Her face lights up like a Christmas tree. "I just want to say seeing you two together makes this old woman's heart feel full. Reminds me of old times, my two kids happy and together."

"That sounds disgusting and illegal," I say as I laugh.

"Good thing I'm not known for my law-abiding tendencies," Cross chimes in, looking at me out of the corner of this eye.

Mom and I laugh as I punch him in the arm. He feigns injury, shaking his bicep back and forth.

"Stop it," I say, shaking my head.

"You have a terrible punch. It's embarrassing."

"What? If that's embarrassing, it's your fault."

"How do you figure?" That grin still plays on his lips.

"You're the one who taught me to punch!"

"Oh, no," he says, pressing his lips together. "I didn't teach you that. Don't blame that crap on me." He captures my gaze, his eyes sparkling. "If you want me to teach you *again*, I'm happy to."

"I don't really punch people a lot."

"Never know," he teases. "You wouldn't want to rest on those laurels."

"You're an ass."

He pretends to consider this as he circles me and heads to the gate. "Trash is out, Brenda. Fixed the latch on the shed—try not to break it again."

"I'll do my best," she promises. "Want to come in for dinner? I brought home Carlson's."

He stops at the gate and looks at me over his shoulder. My heart skips a beat as I watch him make up his mind. I wish I could ask him to stay, wish I could enjoy our banter for a little while longer, but as he looks back at my mother, I know I'm better off if he says no.

"I have a private session in fifteen minutes with a client. I better go, but thanks for the offer." With a final look at me, he opens the gate. "See ya around, Kallie girl."

I hope so.

Chapter 5

Cross

A beer slides across the bar in front of me, stopping only when it hits a set of hands at the end. Machlan's brother, Walker, snaps it up and shoots me a curious look.

"How's it goin'?" he asks, sitting on the stool next to me.

"It's goin'."

"That good, huh?" He takes a long, steady gulp of alcohol before letting the bottle plunk against the wooden bar top. "Peck took a last-minute job at the shop tonight and I'm just getting out of there."

"Should've left him there with it," I offer.

"Yeah, but he had to jack this piece of shit up in the air and, my luck, I leave and it falls on him or something." Giving me a frustrated glance, he takes another drink. "In retrospect, may not have been a terrible idea."

Peeling at the label of my own bottle, I feign interest in the television. It does no good.

"Not that I give a fuck, but what's wrong?" Walker asks.

"Not a damn thing you want to hear about."

"That's true, and I don't even know what it is." He grins. "But,

Machlan is keeping his distance, so that means it might be interesting."

"It's not."

His chest rumbles with a silent chuckle before downing the rest of his brew. I consider getting up and heading to the pool tables in the back just to get some privacy. If I thought it would actually work, I'd try it, but it won't—not with this bunch.

Machlan and I grew up with his brothers, Walker and Lance, and their cousins, Peck and Vincent. We were all close in age and have been tight since preschool.

If I get up and head to the back, Walker will signal Machlan over and he'll tell him what's going on. Walker will rib me for a minute, and if I'm lucky, Peck and Lance won't join in. Walker will then proceed to tell me I'm a dumbass while giving me some token of advice.

The problem? I don't need advice. I need a damn smack to the side of the head.

Running my hand down my face, frustration jumps back into the driver's seat of my life. My stomach twists, sloshing the two beers I've nursed since I came in this evening.

"Okay, I won't play dumb. I know Kallie's back," Walker says, stopping for a moment to acknowledge a woman who stopped to whisper something in his ear. Once she's gone, he turns back to me, but now he's sidetracked. "That's the problem with the world right there."

My gaze trails after the girl I've seen work in the post office then I refocus it on Walker. "What? Easy pieces of ass with great legs?"

"Yup." He motions for Machlan to bring him another beer. "Those girls ruin it for everyone."

"I don't follow you."

"Good idea," Peck says, slipping onto the stool on the other side of Walker. "Don't follow him. This fucker will lead you astray."

"Seriously?" Walker looks at his cousin out of the corner of his eye. "When have I led anyone astray?"

"I think I need to join this conversation," Machlan says, handing Walker a beer. "When has Walker led anyone astray? What about the time you added a little engine to my skateboard and the thing bolted then tossed me off the ramp you built in the back yard and I broke my collarbone?"

"That was your fault." Walker laughs. "Your balance is shit. I had forgotten about that." He scratches his chin. "You know, that was really a good concept."

"I remember that," I say, looking at Machlan. "I think my last words to you were 'This is not a good id—' I didn't even get 'idea' out before you were on your ass."

"Face," Peck inserts. "I think he was on his face, legs kicking in the air."

"Which, in a really weird way, takes us back to pieces of ass with great legs," I say, circling back to the original point. "How is that the ruination of the world?"

"Whoever said that, I agree completely," Machlan adds, shoving off the counter. "The better the ass and legs, the leerier I am of a woman. You get those chunky thighs around your face and—*boom!* The next thing you know there's a pink toothbrush next to yours in the bathroom."

Walker laughs. "So is Kallie's toothbrush back in your bathroom, Cross?"

Peck's eyes widen, but he wisely doesn't say anything. Instead, he hops the bar and rummages through the beer cooler. Machlan lectures him on the law, that he can't be on that side of the bar without a license, but Peck doesn't listen. He never does.

"You saw her," Walker states.

"Yeah."

"And?"

I shrug. Twisting the bottle in my hands, I realize Walker may be the best person in the world to get advice from about this after all. "Fine. I saw her today. We talked for a few minutes and then I saw her again when I went by to do a few things for Brenda."

"You have plans to see her again?"

"I don't know. I'd like to. I tried to cast out some bait, but I'm not sure she took it."

He tips back the new bottle, his eyes focused on the television. A vein in his temple pops, and I wonder what he's going to say. It could be anything with this guy. Whatever it is, it'll be what he believes to be the truth. That's all you get from Walker Gibson.

"Well, in my humble opinion, I say don't," he says.

The finality in his tone irks me. "What do you mean?"

"Look, I know you liked her—hell, we all did. She was a cool girl and you spent your entire adolescence glued to her hip. Trust me," he says, staring off into space, "I get that. You have history with her like you never will with anyone else."

"It's not that…"

"It is." He turns his attention back to me. "But don't do that. She left you once. I know that makes me an asshole to say it bluntly like that, but she did it, not me. You tossed that line out there tonight and she didn't take it. That's enough for me right there. Fuck her," he says, bringing the bottle back to his lips.

My jaw sets, the pulsing almost cracking my back teeth. "Easy there."

Peck leans on the countertop and looks at Walker and then at me. "Don't listen to him unless it has an engine and weighs at least a ton."

"Just offering my opinion," Walker says, getting up. He takes his drinks and meanders toward the back of the bar.

"Listen," Peck says, looking at me with his brows tugged together, "he's wrong."

"How the hell do you know?"

"Because my balls aren't the ones that ache so bad I can't see straight." He grins.

"If I were giving myself advice, I'd say to forget it too," I admit. "I see Walker's point. She left when it got hard. She fought with me back then every fucking day over nothing. I couldn't do anything right. But then I think about how many nights I go to bed wondering where she is and how often I miss her. Then it seems stupid to pretend I don't at least want to get to know her again."

"You've answered your own problem."

"How do you figure?"

Peck shakes his head, downing half his bottle. Wiping his mouth with the back of his hand, he sighs. "You said you could pretend, which means..."

"Yeah..."

"You have two options here," he declares. "You can either let this thing go or you can see what you can make out of it. If you pick option one, get over it. You'll have to, but because I know your ass and know you won't just get over it because you haven't since that fight outside of Crave years ago, option two should come with a lot of consideration. You feel me?"

"I feel you."

"Good. Now that's done, I'm going to see what kind of trouble I can get into tonight." He winks before disappearing into the growing crowd of bodies behind me.

I sit for a long while, returning hellos and chiming in to basic chitchat when required. All the while, my mind is replaying the interactions with Kallie from today. With every second that goes by, I feel a burn in my gut grow hotter.

Leaning forward, I grab my wallet out of my pocket and find a twenty. I put it on the counter and set my beer on top of it. "Hey, Mach! I'm out of here," I say, nodding to the money.

"Tell her I said hi." He grins.

"Fuck off. I'm not going to see her." I look down at the money and then back up at him again. "Maybe tomorrow after work."

Machlan laughs. "Make some time in that busy schedule of yours for me. I want to talk business."

"Will do. Later."

"Later."

Chapter 6

Kallie

"You shouldn't be doing this, Kallie." Rolling my eyes as I head across the parking lot, I set my sights on the building nestled between the laundromat and a secondhand store. "Now I'm talking to myself—totally losing it."

My feet stop and I stand on the edge of the curb, peering into the windows of the gym. The early morning sunlight shines through the glass. Cross is standing in the middle of a stretch of blue mats in a sleeveless shirt and a pair of basketball shorts. A short, caramel-haired woman in all spandex stands in front of him. She's facing me, her hands running through the air as she tells Cross a story. He's watching her, his arms folded in front of him, one eyebrow cocked in the air.

My skin suddenly feels too tight, too unforgiving as I try to draw air into my lungs. When her hand rests on the curve of his bicep, I squeeze my car keys so hard that the alarm goes off behind me.

"Shit!" I mumble, twisting around and shoving the keyring toward the parking lot. "Stop it. Stop it!" Pressing the button repeatedly, the frantic beeping finally stops. "Sorry," I call out to a woman and her child as they climb into the car next to mine. She gives me a look like I'm crazy before speeding off.

I take a deep breath as I feel a gaze on my back. Turning around, I see Cross and the woman in the gym are watching me. I contemplate saving some face and fleeing, but Cross is stalking toward me before I can make a break for it.

He shoves the door open, the muscles in his arms flexing as he holds it. "You all right out here?"

"Yeah." I wince, tucking my keys in my pocket. "My alarm is faulty. Probably a recall or something."

"I bet." He tries to hide his amusement, but fails. "Wanna come in? I mean, I'm assuming you weren't coming this way to do laundry."

Blushing, I walk past him and into the gym.

"Do you know Megan McCarter?" he asks.

"I don't think so. I'm Kallie Welch. Nice to meet you."

"You too," she says in a way that lets me know she doesn't think there's anything nice about meeting me at all.

"Wait, McCarter? Are you related to Molly?"

"She's my older sister," she says, eyes glued to Cross. "Want to show me that move one more time? I think I forgot it already."

"If you forgot it already, you aren't going to remember it next week either," he replies. "I think that's it for us today. Good work."

"I..." She looks at me, then back at Cross. "See you next week."

We wait as she takes her time gathering her things, including a glittery pink water bottle, and heads out. Once the room is free of her noxious perfume, Cross speaks.

"What brought you down here?"

It's the question I asked myself on the car ride here, the one I still haven't answered. All I know is I thought of him all evening and dreamed of him last night. There was no awkwardness in my dream, no feelings of anything other than happiness. I woke up wondering how much of that was just the dream and how much of that was reality. It was hard to tell the two apart.

Shrugging, I look around the room. One half is set up like a gym with treadmills and free weights, and the other has mats and a makeshift boxing ring elevated in the corner. The walls are white with posters of motivational sayings hanging here and there. It's impressive.

"Guess I just wanted to see what you were up to," I say finally. "Is this place yours?"

"Yeah. I opened it a couple of years ago. Have another one in Fairview too."

"Really?" Turning a small circle, I take in every little detail. "That's amazing. Is it just a gym?"

"Just a gym." He snorts, heading to the mats. "It's definitely not *just* a gym, thank you."

"How do I know?"

"You don't, until you ask." He winks. "It *is* a gym. People pay a membership fee to use the facilities, but I also train a couple of amateur fighters and have a boxing program for kids. That's really my favorite thing. They love it for the love of the art, you know? Not because they can whip ass in a bar or flex around town."

"You used to do both things," I point out, moseying my way toward him.

Leaning against a wall, his face sobers. "I did. I still do, if it's warranted, but that's not what I'm about anymore."

The way he speaks the words, the level of sincerity in his tone...it has my heart swelling in my chest. It's a reminder that I don't quite know this man anymore and it raises a host of questions, including how different he just may be now than he was when I left.

"What are you about these days, Cross?"

"I've settled down some, I suppose. Don't interface with the law much these days." He grins. "I work a lot, either here or over at the Fairview gym. I do some online coaching and personal training sessions."

"Like with Megan?"

He shoves off the wall, a twinkle in his eye. "Like Megan," he goads. "Did that bother you?"

"What? Megan? No," I insist, brushing it off. "Why would it?"

"Just an inkling."

"Your inkling would be wrong. How is it my place to have any feelings about what you do in your business?"

"It's not."

It's a simple statement, two little words that pack so much of a punch. *It's not.* It's not the words that irritate me so much; it's the reason for needing them. Even as I stand here inside his gym, even though I feel this link to Cross and have since I saw him yesterday inside Crave, he's nothing more to me than somebody I used to know.

"I don't train many women," he says, picking up a couple of towels along the mats. "I only agreed to three sessions with Megan because someone bought them for her birthday. She has one more and then it's over."

"You aren't training her any more than that?"

"Nah. She knows it. It's ridiculous, really. She doesn't want to know how to box any more than I want to know how to bake a cake."

Laughing at his analogy, I grab a few dumbbells off the floor and put them back in the rack. "I'm glad you found something to do with your life that makes you happy. I always worried you'd float around and get stuck doing something you hated."

"Come on," he teases. "You were really worried I'd end up in jail or on your couch."

"True." I giggle, turning to face him. "But I like this version of you, all grown up."

"Well..." He blows out a breath. "You can thank yourself for that. If you'd have stayed here, I don't think I ever would've realized what a punk I was."

"You weren't a punk."

"I was. I did whatever I wanted and had no plan for going anywhere. Then you left and I realized..." He looks at me and then at the floor. "I realized I'd already lost the best thing that would ever happen to me."

There isn't a reply to that. I just hold a breath and watch his beautiful eyes soften.

"So," he goes on, "one night I decided I was going to do something with myself, and if you ever came back, maybe I could show you I wasn't a loser."

"What if I never came back?"

"Honestly? I'd have been a little relieved."

"Gee, thanks."

"What?" He chuckles, motioning for me to follow him. "Is it wrong that I would've found relief in knowing I wouldn't be falling in love again? That shit hurts, Kal."

I stop walking. "What if I did come back?"

He pauses too and turns around. Running a hand through his thick, silky locks, his cheeks redden. "Then I'd fight like hell to get you back."

"You're just being charming again," I whisper, knowing it's a lie as soon as I say it. There's no denying the stripped-down emotion on his face, the crinkle in his forehead just between his eyes. The corners of his lips flicker, almost pulling into a smile, but not quite.

"Come on," he says, turning away. "Let's teach you how to throw a punch."

Chapter 7
Kallie

"I like this one too." I point at the screen toward a small one-bedroom, one-bathroom apartment.

"It's so small," Nora remarks. "That bathroom is barely big enough to turn around in."

"True. But it'll be just me. I don't need tons of space."

"If you use more than five cosmetics at one time, you're screwed. Just think about that."

Nora sinks into the pillows on her sofa as I readjust the computer on my lap. We've been at this for a while now and my friend's patience is running thin—not because of the house hunt. Because I've not brought up Cross.

Just thinking about him in theory alone causes my stomach to go crazy and, when I allow my brain to focus on his face or his smell or his touch, it's lights out. I can't focus on anything else. It's a Cross Show and I don't necessarily want a ticket.

Nora does, though. Her gaze is heavy on the side of my face as I pretend to be immersed in the hunt for an apartment.

"What about this one?" I ask.

"Stop ignoring me."

"What are you talking about? I'm talking to you. That's hardly ignoring you." I laugh, feigning ignorance.

She sighs dramatically. "You aren't giving me an opening."

"An opening for what?"

Scrambling to sit up, she throws a pillow at me. "I know you saw Cross."

My head falls to the cushion at my back. Just like that, the weight that had been sitting on top of us is now squarely on my shoulders. I close the computer lid. "And how do you know that?"

"I saw your car at the gym. I just happened to be heading to Crank to take Walker and Peck a sandwich and saw it there." Her bottom lip juts out. "You didn't even call me."

Laughing, I lift my head. "I don't have to call you with every little thing, Nora."

"This is not a little thing! You saw Cross. Privately. Alone."

"And it was private," I say, shaking my head. "Do you know what that means?"

"Yup. It means it's for the two of you and me. Besides," she says, rolling her eyes, "everyone knows. Machlan asked me about it while we were closing tonight."

"Oh, good grief." I groan.

My eyes close as I prepare to either answer or do my best to deflect her questions. But, when the peace is supposed to come, Cross's handsome face comes instead. I feel a smile inch across my lips as my insides grow warm.

My hips sing as the memory of his hands gripping them yesterday as he showed me how to punch again lights up my mind. The heat of his breath on the back of my neck. The wicked combination of tenderness and ferocity that danced in his eyes.

It's only natural to be almost-smitten already with him, but it's also irresponsible. I'm not a child anymore, hardly the teenager that fell in love with a boy a couple of years older than her with the crooked grin.

I need to adult this relationship. *Potential relationship.* Letting my walls come down without realizing my fears are still absolutely warranted would be careless. And stupid. And so, so easy.

"So?" she prods.

"So, what?" I ask. "Yes, I saw him. He's ..."

She watches me carefully, not saying a word. I don't either. I have no idea where to go with this statement. I could say he's more handsome than he was when I left. It'd be honest to say I didn't want to leave him last night. I'd be lying if I said I'm happy he didn't kiss me or that the look in his eye didn't make me feel all sorts of things. All of that would be true.

But I could also tell her I was up all night worrying about it. That it's all too soon. That I've been poked enough in the last year between my job and my ex-boyfriend to want to get into anything serious again. Especially with Cross. One toe in with him is as good as diving in headfirst and I don't need that risk.

"Come on, Kal," she says. "I know him. I know you. I know him and you together."

"No, you don't." I set the computer on the table in front of me to mask the epic gulp of air I take. "I don't even know who he is or who I am, let alone who the two of us are together."

"That's not true. I've been your best friend all these years plus I've been around to watch him. Maybe the part about me not knowing you two together now is kinda true, but I can imagine." She swipes her thumb over her lips. "So, you still love him."

"No," I insist, swinging my head side to side emphatically. "I don't. Stop that."

She holds her hands in front of her, signaling she's done with that line of questioning but the harm is done.

So, you still love him.

My feet beg to hit the floor and pace a good, solid circle to get rid of some of the energy bursting through my veins. Instead, I fiddle with a piece of fringe on the pillow next to me. It's less panicked-looking.

I'd always hoped if I saw Cross again that it wouldn't feel like the

Fourth of July. That somehow, I wouldn't be drawn to him like a sunset to a horizon. I told myself it would be like meeting any other man I'd known and would prove the thing between us was just a juvenile obsession.

Damn hopes, anyway.

"He's all grown up now," Nora says, like she needs to point that out. She laughs when I give her a blank stare. "Maybe things could work out."

"I don't want them to. Not with Cross, not with anyone." My feet hit the floor and I scamper across the room. "I want to breathe, Nora. I want to not worry about someone else and their life and how their decisions might impact me. I want to just do what I want to do for once."

"So ... do Cross."

"Nora!"

She giggles in response. "Sometimes I hate they all feel like family to me. Except Lance," she says, referring to Machlan's other brother. "I'd do Lance but now he has Mariah so that's out."

"You need a man."

"Oh no." She laughs, getting to her feet too. "We're not turning this around on me. We're talking about you here."

Hands on my hips, I take in Nora's amused grin. She finds this entertaining; all she can see is the happy at the end. I know better. I know the feeling, quite vividly, of the doldrums of a relationship, with Cross specifically, and that happy is a hard-fought battle to win —if it can be won at all.

That's what really scares me. What if you have to settle in life? What if you can't really ever be totally satisfied in a relationship? What if you never have the confidence in yourself, or them, or you together to not go to sleep with a nagging in your gut?

What if the stars never align like you hope as a little girl?

"What is it, Kallie?" she asks, her grin faltering.

"Is it fair to just be ... scared?"

"Of what?"

"Of ... life? Of falling in love." I gulp. "Of trying and not getting the things I want out of life?"

"Where's all this coming from?" she whispers. "What's going on?"

I plop into the chair next to me and take in a long, deep breath. "I've been thinking a lot about things. Life, I guess. Think about it," I tell her. "What are the odds you'll find someone that has the same goals as you? The same dreams? Enough love for you to want to see you do the things you want to do? It's not good, Nora."

"People do it every day," she says, sitting on the arm of the chair.

"No, people settle every day. Look around at the people you know. Most of them settle. They take what's available out of fear they won't have what they really want and they're halfway miserable their whole life. That was me with my ex. I realized that too late and wasted way too long."

"Okay," she says like I've lost my mind. "What makes you happy? Let's start there."

"I don't know."

Her hands go in the air as she laughs. "I quit."

"Good," I say, partially relieved and partially wishing she'd press the issue for once.

"Let's go get milkshakes."

"Fine. But you're buying."

Cross

I add a scoop of protein powder to the blender, put the cap back on, and press the button. It whirls, the contents of the glass container smashing around with no fucks given, kind of like my brain. It's like a box full of noisy items in the hands of a toddler. Everything is banging around.

Busying myself with pouring the drink into a cup, I whistle as I work. The house seems so quiet. Too quiet, even, to do the usual bookkeeping for the gyms or research exercises as I usually do. It's too quiet for anything.

I lean against the counter and take a gulp of my drink. The glass leaves a dampness on my palm, the remaining ice chunks rattling around in the mixture. I hold it to the light and laugh. It's light grayish in color just like my favorite set of eyes.

Damn it.

The cup hits the counter with a thud.

"What are you gonna do now?" I ask myself. "'Cause you're gonna have to do something."

Rolling my shoulders around, trying to work out the stress captured at the base of my neck, I head into the living room toward the sound of my ringing cell phone. "Hello?" I ask.

"Hey, big brother," Hadley chirps through the line. "How are you?"

"All right. What are you up to?"

She sighs. "What's wrong?"

"Nothing. Why?" I ask. I watch as the neighbor's kids kick a ball back and forth on the other side of the road.

"I hear it in your voice. You're … *blah.*"

"I've never been described as *blah.*" I laugh.

"You have now." She giggles. "So, what's up?"

The ball goes back and forth. The little girl rockets it across the lawn and the boy misses, his leg sweeping right over the top before he falls to the ground.

I feel for him. I have half a notion to head over there and help him up and give him some advice on being ready for the hardest shot. To always protect yourself. To never let your guard down.

Especially with girls.

"Kallie is in town." I say it as easily as I can, as if it's no big deal that the girl I've been torn up over for years has reappeared. My sister, though, doesn't need all the bells and whistles to signal an issue. She knew Kallie. She knows me.

"Well, I wasn't expecting that," she mutters.

"That would make two of us."

"Have you seen her? Like, just the two of you?"

"Yeah."

"And? How'd it go?"

As the little boy gets back to his feet by way of a proffered hand from the little girl, I turn away from the window. "It went better than I expected in some ways and a little worse in others."

Hadley pauses. "How is she?"

"Good. Beautiful. What else can I say?" I sigh. "This is harder than I thought it would be."

"It's never easy to see someone you love—or loved," she adds quickly. "There's always that feeling of what could've been."

"Talking about Machlan?" I tease.

"No, I'm not talking about Machlan," she mocks ... and lies. "I know what that would've been. A big, ridiculous mess."

"Sure about that?"

"Absolutely."

With a snort at how confident she doesn't sound, I head back toward the kitchen. My stomach rolls the protein shake over. It has nothing to do with the ingredients, though, and everything to do with the topic of conversation.

I've been with a number of women since Kallie left. A lot of them, really. And at the end of the night when they'd leave my house or I'd pull on my jeans and leave theirs, I'd do one thing immediately: take a shower. The smell of a woman on my skin drove me insane. It didn't matter how hot she was or how much I did or didn't like her, she didn't belong on me. It was like my skin itched with the scent of her until I sent it down the shower drain.

I'd kill for Kallie's shampoo to be on my shirt. Her perfume mixed with my body oils, her kisses lingering on my skin.

The more I think about it, the more panicked I get. I want it too much. Hell, I've always wanted it. I've always wanted *her*. And now that she's here and I realize nothing has changed in that regard, it's scary as fuck.

"Hadley? Let me ask you a question."

"Shoot."

"Let's pretend for one second that Machlan's not Machlan."

"Yeah right." She laughs.

"No, really. Play along."

She groans. "Fine."

"What if you were the problem between you and a guy—"

"It's Machlan's fault," she interrupts immediately.

"But this isn't Machlan ..."

"Oh, yeah. Continue."

Laughing, I wipe my hand over my face. "Okay. This guy, not Machlan, and you were together. And it was your fault. And now he's back and he's giving you the time of day, which you didn't expect, and all you can think about is getting him back. But you—"

"Go get her," she interrupts again. "Just go see her. No expectations because you were the problem in that relationship."

"Gee, thanks."

"You know it. I'm not going to lie to you."

Blowing out a breath, I look at the ceiling. "What if it's just that she's so familiar to me, Had? What if we broke up for a reason and I'm an idiot to want something again? I mean, I don't even know her these days. What if I'm relying on this idea I've had in my head all these years?"

"Then you go get her, like I told you. Take her to lunch. Take her for a walk," she says. "Just spend some time with her. If it's some stupid crush from back in the day, you'll toss her out like you do the rest of the whores from the bar."

"Be nice," I tease.

"I'm not about to be nice," she states. "Crave is the worst thing to happen to you and Machlan Gibson ever."

A smile tickles my lips. "I thought we weren't talking about Machlan."

"We aren't. I gotta go. I have a date with a guy that isn't an egotistical bar owner."

"Oh, the pudfucker I met? The one that looks like he has a corncob stuck up his ass?"

"He's nice, Cross. You should be happy I met a nice guy."

"You met a pussy, that's what you did. He's your version of a bar whore."

"I met him in a library," she deadpans.

"Okay. Book whore."

"That's not how you use that term." She laughs.

"It's a term? I thought I made it up." I shrug.

"You didn't. And I gotta go. Have a good night, brother."

"You, too, Had."

"Night."

"Night."

Chapter 8

Cross

It's a gamble, a big risk, one I'm not entirely sure is going to pay off, but one I feel absolutely certain about making. My conversation with Hadley last night put a few things in perspective and, although I'd never tell her she might be right, she might really be. It's worth a shot, anyway.

Taking the steps two at a time, I press my finger on the doorbell. Footsteps fall against the hardwood floors on the other side before the door pulls open.

My chest fills like it does every time I see Kallie. I fight the stupid smile that plays on my lips, but it's no use—I'm grinning like a fucking loon.

"Hey," she says, her fingers playing at the hem of her shirt. "What are you doing here?"

"Well, I was driving by Carlson's a bit ago and saw they had Cobb salad on the sign. I thought maybe we could grab a bite to eat."

"You remember that I like Cobb salad?"

"With extra avocado and bacon, no egg, right?"

Her eyes light up as she grins. "Yeah." She laughs. "That's right."

"So, wanna go?"

She looks over her shoulder before turning her attention back to me. "Um, sure. Let me get my shoes and purse and I'll meet you outside, okay?"

"Sounds good."

In a few minutes, we're sitting in the cab of my pickup and heading down the road.

"My shoulders are sore," she says, working her arm in a circle. "How do you punch all day and still have use of your extremities?"

"You get used to it. Do it long enough and your muscles get built up."

"That explains a lot."

I look at her quickly before turning my attention back to the road. "That explains what?"

"Your arms," she gushes, wrapping a hand around my bicep. "They're ridiculous, Cross, and your back. Is that from boxing?"

"Been checking me out?" I love that she's looked hard enough to take notice.

"No. Well, yeah." She smirks. "It's kind of hard not to. You look good."

"And here I thought it was my charm drawing you in."

She smacks my arm before pulling her hand away. "Your charm is better, but it's still not your forte."

"So you only want me for my body? That's what you're saying?" I joke.

"No!"

"I mean, it's okay. I have no problem being wanted for my body—none. I'll strip right now if it'll help."

"You're too much."

Chuckling, I pull the truck into the parking lot of Carlson's. We climb out and meet at the front then, without thinking, I take her hand in mine. Her small palm is delicate and fits inside mine like it was designed for this purpose alone. I expect her to pull it away, but much to my surprise, she just looks up at me and smiles.

Once inside, we take a seat next to the front windows. Before I can get a word out, Veronica is halfway across the building. "Kallie Welch!" she squeals. "I haven't seen you in ages!"

"Hi, Veronica." Kallie gets to her feet and greets Veronica with a hug. "How are you?"

"Better now that I've seen you," she says as Kallie settles back in. "Where have you been? Are you home now?"

"Yeah, I'm home now. Cross saw you had Cobb salad on the menu for today and picked me up."

Veronica raises a brow. "I see. You and Cross back together, huh?"

"Oh, no," Kallie replies quickly, shaking her head. "No, not like that."

"And why not? Have you seen this boy lately? He's a catch, Kal. Every girl in town has tried their hand with this one."

"Should I walk away for a while? Because this is a little awkward with me sitting right here." I chuckle.

"Every girl, huh?" Kallie puts her face in her hands and watches me. "Do tell."

Shaking my head, I grab a menu out of the holder and flip my attention to the words on the plastic. "I'll have a ham and Swiss on sourdough, cheddar and sour cream chips, and a pop. Kallie?"

"Cobb salad, extra avocado and bacon, no egg, and a water."

Veronica disappears into the back after whispering into Kallie's ear. Once she's gone, I breathe a sigh of relief. "So..."

"So..." she says, taking my menu and sliding it back in its spot. "Did you have a lot of clients today?"

"None as fun as you," I say with a wink.

"Oh, I bet. I was a barrel of fun."

"What did you do today?" I ask, watching the sun stream onto her face. It creates a halo effect around her blonde hair, which seems fitting.

"I had breakfast with Nora. Ran into Peck at Goodman's—he hasn't changed a bit."

"Nope. He's the same thirteen-year-old boy he always was."

She laughs, relaxing back in her seat. "I hope he never changes. He's so sweet and kind and handsome."

"Do I have competition?"

She doesn't answer, just rolls her eyes.

Plates of food are set down in front of us, Veronica making small talk with Kallie about her mother and once upon a time when Kallie worked at Carlson's. I don't touch my sandwich. Instead, I watch the girl in front of me act like she hasn't been gone a day. On the other hand, it seems like she's a completely different person.

Her old soul is still there; that hasn't changed. It's one of the first things I fell in love with. Her ability to think clearly and make good, solid choices was something I couldn't do, and it drew me in like a magnet. It didn't hurt that she was gorgeous, made straight As, and was the captain of the cheerleading team.

She was also too sweet, too forgiving. I took that for granted like a young, dumb motherfucker.

"What?" she asks, catching me staring.

"I was just thinking about you."

She stabs a chunk of avocado and pops it in her mouth. "What about me?"

"Wondering why you really came home."

She chews slowly, as if biding her time. The lines around her eyes crease as she considers her response. "I told you," she says, pausing to take a drink of water. "My job got a little crazy and Sky moved. It was the right time."

"That's not true."

"How do you know?"

Setting my fork down on the side of my plate, I rest my elbows on the table. "You don't have to tell me anything you don't want to. I don't care, as long as you're safe and you're here. That's all that really matters."

"I'm fine, Cross. Safe and here," she says, extending her arms to the side as if to say, *Look! Here we are!* "Maybe I just..." Her arms fall to her sides and she takes a gulp of air. "Maybe I got tired."

My heart twists in my chest and I reach for her hand. She allows me to take it. I turn it over, palm up, and press my thumb in the middle.

"I'm not complaining," she says quietly. "I don't want it to come across as a pity party, but I'm just *tired*. I've worked my ass off since I was fifteen years old."

"I know. No one can ever say you're a slacker."

"Not with a straight face." She sighs. "I loved my job in Indy. It was exciting and challenging and something different every day. When my boss was indicted, it shook me to the core. I had no idea he was doing anything wrong," she insists. "All of a sudden, what little time I did have was spent with investigators, telling them everything I knew so I didn't get in trouble too." She takes a napkin off the table and dots the corner of her eye. "I couldn't eat, couldn't sleep. My stomach was in knots. I remember sitting on my bed one night at three AM and just thinking, 'Why am I doing this?'"

Squeezing her hand, it takes everything I have in me not to bolt around the table and sweep her up in my arms.

Her chin dips down as she removes her hand from beneath mine. I want to snatch it back up, pull her over the table and onto my lap, and kiss the hell out of her.

As I watch her mind go elsewhere, mine goes back to the original question. "That all makes total sense," I say carefully. "But it's not enough to make you uproot your life."

She lifts a brow.

"It's not," I insist. "I know you. Something else happened. What was it?"

Leaning back in her seat, she shakes her head. "Everyone else just took the story and ran with it. Why can't you?"

"Because I know you?" I offer, suppressing a chuckle. "Because that look in your eyes wasn't put there by some boss who did something stupid and caused all these problems."

She watches me for a long moment, the internal war she fighting plain as day on her face. Finally, she rushes out a breath and leans forward. "My boyfriend cheated on me, okay?"

"Boyfriend?" I ask, lifting a brow.

"*Ex*-boyfriend," she corrects. "Look, it's not a big deal. Yeah, it bruised my ego a little but—"

"I'd love to see the girl he cheated on you with." I laugh, not even trying to hide my amusement. "Or maybe it was a guy—that would make more sense."

"Cross!"

"I mean it. There's not a woman better than you in the entire world. Maybe there's a guy." I shrug. "I wouldn't know because I'm not looking over there."

"But you're looking at women?"

"Don't distract me," I admonish, wagging a finger in the air. "That's not what we're discussing."

"Maybe it's what I want to discuss."

"Too fucking bad." I grin. "So, some asshole broke your heart?"

A shadow drifts across her face as her features soften. "That was a few years ago," she almost whispers. "This guy just hurt my feelings."

I shouldn't want to smile at that, but I do anyway. It should incense me that I broke her heart, but I've had a few years to deal with that guilt. All I can process from that sentence is what I can read between the lines, and that shit makes me happy.

She wasn't in love with him.

"Yeah, well, you know what they say." I shrug.

"What's that?"

"If you break something, it's your responsibility to fix it."

"If you break something, you're generally not trusted with it again," she tosses back.

"Oh, come on," I scoff. "That's like telling a man he's not allowed to eat off the good china because he broke a plate when he was a baby."

She makes a face. "That's a terrible analogy."

"Whatever. You know what I mean, and I know just what you need tonight."

"I bet you do," she says, narrowing her eyes. "One track mind, Cross?"

Grinning, I lean forward. "I think we have two different things we're thinking of, but by the look in your eye, I'm more than happy to go with yours."

"What are you thinking?"

Picking up my sandwich, I take a bite. "Eat up. Then I'll show you."

Chapter 9
Kallie

"Oh my God," I squeal, bouncing in the seat of Cross's truck. "Storybook Village! I thought they shut this place down!"

The truck slides into a spot in front of a cutout of a giant shoe. I take in the ducks waddling around and the smell of manure as the engine stops.

"They did," Cross says. "I think it was down when you left."

"It was. It hadn't been open for a few years."

"Well, this guy named Charlie bought it and opened it back up, last summer, I think. I thought maybe we could play a round of putt-putt."

Like a kid on Christmas morning, I clap my hands. "You're going down, Cross."

"We'll see, Kallie girl."

We get out of the truck and enter through the little doorway where the frame around it is painted like a pirate ship. This was where our class had our senior pictures taken because we'd all spent so much time here in the summers growing up.

Storybook Village was a small-town version of an amusement park. The only ride was a little train Paul would start up when enough people were visiting, and it took you on a tour of the entire setup.

Growing up, this was as good as going to a far-off country. There were peacocks and giraffes, a bear and a tiger. I could spend all day milling around, feeding the ducks handfuls of corn, then ending the day with a round of mini golf.

"Nice to see you, Cross," an older lady says as we enter the little check-in area.

"How are you, Maggie?"

"Good, honey. I'm good. What can I do for you?"

"Two for a round of putt-putt," he says, placing a twenty on the desk. "I'm gonna show this girl how it's done, Mags."

"Whatever," I scoff, picking out a pink ball. "He doesn't know what's about to hit him."

Maggie laughs candidly as she sorts through a bag of change. Handing Cross the difference, she tells us to grab our equipment and start through the door on the left.

The afternoon sun is warm as we step into the golfing area, and a giant plastic giraffe greets us.

"Do you remember when Peck tried to climb up the legs and get a picture taken on its back?" I laugh. "I thought old man Paul was going to have a heart attack."

"I forgot about that. Do you remember when Machlan tried to capture a peacock? And it trashed the hell out of his arm?" Cross laughs. "Apparently it was mating season and the male thought he was competition for his woman."

We exchange smiles as I set my ball on the little circle to start. One crack of the club and it misses the blade of a giant pinwheel, making it to the other side through a little tunnel. With one more putt, I'm in the cup.

"Beat that," I say, marking me down for two strokes.

He takes his green ball and sets it on the tee. The club looks so tiny in his hands, and he almost bends in half to take a swing. Once he does, the ball rips through the tunnel, runs a circle around the rim of the cup, and sinks in.

"Dammit." Narrowing my eyes, I head to the second hole. "You got lucky."

Lining up my ball, I get into position to hit it. Before I do, I feel him behind me. My heart flutters in my chest like it has the wings of a butterfly. Holding my breath, I wait as I feel his proximity grow near, my body pulled to his like there's an invisible wire connecting us, reeling me in.

"You're right," he whispers, his breath hot against the shell of my ear. "I did get lucky."

Instinctively, I sag backward, my back resting against his chest. It takes about half a second for his arms to wrap around my waist, pulling me into him. His face finds the crook of my neck and he breathes in, the air trickling over my sensitive skin and making me shiver.

The air is saturated with the scent of his cologne, infiltrating my senses and making me lightheaded. I grab his arms where they're locked at my belly to steady myself. His forearms are roped, thick with muscle, his skin coarse against my fingers.

A flood of emotions comes raring back. Suddenly, I'm reminded of the uncertainty of him staying out all night with Machlan, of being rumored to be with another girl every other Friday night, of him showing up late for everything and his failure to get a job.

Cross sweeps the hair off the back of my neck and presses a soft kiss just above my shoulder.

"Cross?"

"Yeah?"

"Can I trust you?"

He presses another kiss to the same spot before raising his face and resting his chin on the top of my head. "You can never go by what someone says to that question, Kal. You have to go with your gut."

It's the right answer, but it's no help. I don't know what in the world my gut is saying. I can hear my brain, feel my heart, experience the throb between my legs, but my gut? No clue.

He moves slightly behind me, just enough so his hardness presses into my back. I gulp, the length rock solid as he stills.

Everything picks up pace, my sensations overloading as I run my hands up his forearms and close my eyes. There's not a thing about this moment that feels wrong or out of place, not one single thing that screams at me to stop or reconsider.

"How dedicated are you to finishing this game of golf?" I ask, subtly pressing my ass against him.

"All I want is a hole in one."

Spinning around, I catch the grin on his lips. "That's a terrible line."

"Can't win 'em all." He laughs. "Ready to get out of here?"

"Depends on where we're going."

His gaze drags down my body, blazing a trail as he works his way back up to my eyes. Licking his lips, he takes the club out of my hands. "My house is closer."

"What are we waiting for?"

———

Kallie

The door creaks as Cross twists the knob and presses it open. We enter, stepping into a little foyer that has dark hardwood floors and beige walls. He's decorated the place sparsely, with few pictures and little else.

"Live here long?" I ask, looking at the three little images framed near the doorway to the living room. There's one of him and Machlan on their high school graduation day, another of him and the Gibson boys at Bluebird Hill in the middle of winter. The last one is of himself, one hand raised in the air at a boxing match. "I remember that," I tell him, pointing to the last one. "You won by knockout."

"I did," he says, placing a hand on my hip. "You were there, two rows up."

"You were so good. I'd never seen anything like that before. So controlled, so careful."

"So not like me every other minute of my life, huh?"

Turning to see him, I cup his cheek in my hand. "That's what confused me so much. You were so talented, so cautious. Then outside the ring, you were the opposite."

"In the ring," he says, pulling his brows together, "someone cared. My trainer wouldn't let me get by with crap or acting like an idiot, but outside of the ring, no one cared."

"I cared."

"Maybe a part of me thought you shouldn't."

"Maybe...maybe I should've cared more."

"Oh, no," he says, sweeping an arm under my legs and picking me up in a bridal carry. "We're not going down that road."

He carries me with ease, a teasing grin on his face as we walk down a blank hallway and into a room at the end. There's a huge bed with silver-grey blankets and more pillows than any one person should ever need. Instead of laying me down easily, he tosses me into the center. I bounce as I hit, sending a few pillows toppling to the floor.

Everything smells like a mixture of his cologne and soap, a scent I could fall asleep and wake up to with no problem, a scent that reminds me of Cross. It's a scent that warms my heart.

His phone begins to ring and he pulls it from his pocket. After a quick glance, he holds the side until it stops and then tosses it on a dresser. A few seconds later, he's stretched out his long frame beside me.

"Was that important?" I ask as he rolls over on his side to look at me.

"Nope. Nothing is more important than you in my bed right

now." One hand rests against my stomach, just below my breasts. He tenses his fingers and they press lightly into my skin. "I'm going to kiss you."

"It's about time," I tease, my breath coming out in ragged heaps.

"I'm warning you, because once I start, I won't be able or willing to stop. It's a very slippery slope."

He's giving me an out. I do a quick internal inventory, looking for a reason to get up and walk out. There's nothing to warrant that, but there are a hundred reasons to reach over and wrap my hand along the back of his neck. I guide his head toward mine, and our lips touch.

Immediately, every muscle in my body relaxes, every care in the world dissolving under his touch. His lips move tenderly, but there's an undercurrent of possession that is undeniable. It's freeing to be in his hold, to know that it's him guiding me, protecting me, because if there's one thing about Cross I've never once felt unsure about, it's that he'd never let anything happen to me.

Being with other men was never like this. It was a mess of awkward touches, weird hang-ups, and a strange dance between the two of us that demonstrated how unsure, how wrong we were with one another.

I lie on his bed, his body hovering over me, his lips kissing every thought and feeling into mine. Our mouths move together, mine opening, his tongue slipping right past my lips, as if this is the way things are supposed to be.

Lifting the hem of his shirt, I drag it up and over his head. He breaks the kiss just long enough to let the fabric rush by then crashes his mouth to mine again. The silky strands of his hair glide through my fingers, the stubble on his cheeks roughing up my palms as I find every way possible to make contact with his body.

The muscles of his back flex as he moves off me, the lines in his sides stretching as he climbs off the bed and to his feet. He grins salaciously, panting as hard as I am.

"Why do you still have clothes on?" I ask, running my eyes down his tanned, taut skin.

"Why do you?"

I flinch for one brief moment, waiting for the fear I have of getting naked in front of another person to kick in. At that exact second, when I feel the niggle of embarrassment start to work its way in, Cross decides to smile—not the sexy one, the one that makes me want to take off my clothes because my libido is running wild, the other one...the shy one, the one that builds me up in a way that makes me want to be with him. They are two very different things.

Lifting my hips, I skim my shorts down my legs and kick them off. They sail through the air then he catches them with one hand.

"Best answer ever," he says, tossing them to the floor.

"I didn't think you'd mind, but you still have your pants on, and that's a problem."

His chest rumbles with a chuckle as he works his pants and boxers down his body one glorious inch at a time. "It's gonna be a big problem."

I see what he means.

He palms his cock in his hand, the tip of it almost reaching his belly button. It's swollen, ready for me, a bead of pre-cum sitting at the top as he squeezes the shaft.

"It's a good thing," I begin, twisting around on the bed so my feet aren't dangling off the end, "I'm a good problem solver."

The mattress dips with his weight, my skin burning as his swipes against it. He sits back on his knees at my feet and looks down at me. "Promise me one thing."

"What's that?" I ask, my heart pounding in my chest. The way he looks at me steals my breath, knots my stomach into a bundle of emotions I can't begin to unravel right now. It's as if he's not just seeing my body, or my anticipation of his next move. He's seeing me in a way that's bare and has nothing to do with a lack of fabric on my body.

"You'll stay with me for a while tonight."

"Why?"

He plants his hands on either side of me, leaning down just

enough so his chest touches the peaks of my nipples. "Because holding you in my arms is my favorite part."

"Oh, Cross," I whisper, my heart melting on the spot.

Wrapping my legs around his waist, I press my lips to his. He nips at my bottom lip, tugging it between his teeth. I can't stop the moan that escapes my throat as I tilt my hips up to his.

His cock is at my opening, teasing me. It dips in, parting me with its girth before slipping back out again. He does this over and over, swiping at my swollen clit with each pass. His hands cup my breasts, kneading them in his coarse palms.

"I want to touch every inch of you," he whispers, sliding his hands up my chest and across my collarbone. "I need every piece of you to remember it belongs to me."

I whimper, trying to move as he slides into me.

"You've always been mine, just like I've always been yours."

"Yes," I eek out. "Gah!"

He slides inside me, almost like he teased himself too long, like he couldn't wait a second longer to get inside me.

"I'm glad I didn't bother asking if you were ready," he says, closing his eyes as he sinks into me again. "So...damn...wet."

His Adam's apple bobs in his throat, a low guttural groan originating somewhere deep inside. I could almost get off just watching him enjoy me.

Dropping my knees wider, I roll my head to the side to allow him to bury his head in the crook of my neck. "You are so sexy," he whispers through gritted teeth.

"Go deeper," I pant, locking my heels around him. It puts me in a position I know he loves, an angle I know he can't resist.

"God," he groans, thrusting harder. "This feels so good."

"*So good.*"

He kisses me at every possible point, doing just as he promised—touching me in every place he can. He holds my shoulders, pinches a nipple, cups the side of my face, the outside of my thigh, making every possible connection he can between us.

Up, up, up I go, pulled into a swirling state of bliss between the friction of his cock and the sweet words he whispers in my ear. It's a heady mix, a complicated yet simple combination that is as irresistible as he is.

"Cross," I pant, my legs shaking with the impending climax. "I can't...you..."

My eyes squeeze shut with the force of the eruption that's starting to build in the bottom of my belly. Like a slow-burning fire, the heat rolls out to the tops of my thighs, into my chest before radiating into my toes and the top of my head.

"Cross!"

He pounds me into harder, his breath whispering over my skin with each push. He mutters something under his breath, but I can't make it out over my moans.

My body falls apart around him, my mind reeling with an influx of sensations. I feel him tense, his body shifting on top of me before he enters me hard and holds the position with the tip of his cock at the back of my pussy.

As he slips it back out and milks his orgasm, he flutters his eyes open. Instead of the lust I saw a few minutes ago, all I see now is something different, something soft...something I want to hold on to for a very long time.

He presses a soft kiss to my lips before pulling out and settling on the bed beside me. Pulling me into him, he nestles his face into my hair.

"I know you need to get up," he whispers, kissing a spot just above my ear. "But give me a few seconds first, okay?"

As I drift off to sleep, I keep reminding myself to get up and go to the bathroom, but I don't. This feels too good.

Chapter 10

Cross

"**A**re you ready?" I ask.

Taking Kallie's hand, I help her out of my truck. The wind moves little wisps of hair around her face as her feet hit the asphalt. She's gorgeous in cutoff blue jeans and a plain, navy-colored T-shirt. Maybe it's from the shirt—I don't know, but the gray in her eyes almost looks blue tonight.

Her palm rests in mine, her skin soft and warm. I have half a notion to throw her back in the truck and take her home with me, but that's not what tonight is about. Having her in my home, in my bed, for the last couple of days has been a dream come true. Tonight is about showing her how good we are together outside of the bed. Outside the gym. In front of all our friends.

"Are you sure about this?" she asks, looking up at Crave.

"Hell, yeah I'm sure about this." *I'm sure about a lot of things.* I squeeze her hand tighter. "It'll be fun."

The door is pushed open from the inside and a couple exit. I usher Kallie in front of me as a stream of music and laughter fills our ears. My hand rests on the small of her back and I hope she takes it as a sign I'm here for her. In reality, it's to sturdy myself.

My usual ability to stay calm despite the situation is gone. My fingers flex against the fabric of her shirt, my blood pounding through my veins. This is the one thing I've always wanted: my girl walking with me on a mundane Friday night.

Heads turn as we enter and shouts of "Hey, Kallie!" echo over the music. She waves at a few tables of people we know as if she just saw them yesterday. It's as natural as the day is long and a smile tips my lips.

She reaches for my hand. I take it and then tug her, bringing her to a stop. Her back to my chest, I hover my lips near the shell of her ear.

"If you decide you want to leave," I say, my arm going around her and my fingers splaying against her belly, "just say the word."

Her head falls back to my chest as her perfume floods my senses. "Keep it up, bud, and we won't get a chance to sit." She presses her ass backward.

"Kal ..." I growl before her giggle cuts me off.

"Behave, Cross." She flips me a look before heading toward the bar. "Hey, Peck!"

Peck sets a bottle down in front of him and grins. "Hey, Kallie. I'd hug you but I don't want to get knocked out."

"Smart guy," I say, helping Kallie onto a stool next to him before climbing on one myself. "What's happening, Peck?"

"Not much. Just got off work and thought I'd come by and see what I can get into."

"How was Walker today?" I ask.

"The usual." He groans. "On the phone with Sienna. Watching Sienna's ass when she comes in. Texting Sienna. Super fucking annoying."

"Like that wouldn't be you with Molly McCarter," Machlan says, planting his palms on the bar.

Peck tips his bottle Machlan's way. "One day it will be. One day."

"Only if the universe hates you." Machlan winks. Then he turns to Kallie. "Well, if this isn't a sight for sore eyes."

"Better be talking about us together and not her. I'm not above busting your ass, Mach," I say, half-kidding.

He stands straight and holds out his calm, even hand. "I'm shaking."

"Fucker." I laugh.

"How are you tonight, Machlan?" Kallie asks, looking at him sweetly.

"Can't complain. Actually," he says, leaning against the bar, "I'm probably a little better than usual now that you've taken that asshole off my hands." He looks at me and grins.

"Can you get me something to drink?" Kallie asks Machlan.

"Sure. What do you want?"

"I don't know. I don't drink much."

Machlan chuckles. "What level we looking at? Buzzed? Karaoke? One-night stand?"

That last part was for my benefit. I try not to react.

Kallie's hand hits my thigh just a half an inch from my groin. I cup mine over hers and hold it in place.

"Probably buzzed. I don't sing and your buddy here might have something to say if I went with one-night stand."

"Damn right," I say, stroking her hand with my thumb.

"I vote for the one-night stand," Peck chimes in.

"Peck? Today's not the day," I warn.

He peers at me around Kallie. "And why is that?"

"I told you to behave," Kallie says, swatting at me. "I'm going to use the ladies' room. Is Nora around?"

"She's in the back talking to Kip." Machlan rolls his eyes.

"What did she do?" Kallie asks, mouth hanging open. "Kip is the sheriff now, right?"

"I'd guess she did him." Machlan snorts. "I just stay away from the store room when he needs to debrief her."

Kallie makes a face as she gets off the stool. "Ew. Okay. I'll avoid that area. Be right back."

I watch her walk away, ignoring Peck's comments. She stops a few times and says hello to random people and it's all I can do not to follow her."

"You got it bad," Machlan says, pulling my attention away from the bathroom door.

"Nah," I say, taking the beer bottle from him.

Machlan taps the top of the bar and ventures to the far side to take an order.

Once he's gone, Peck leans toward me, twisting his cap around backward. The typical goofball look on his face is gone. It's replaced with one that has me biting my lip.

"She's a good girl. I know you know that," he says.

"Then why are you telling me?"

He grins. "You know she left before because you were a shithead, right?"

"Again, not sure why you're telling me this," I say, taking a swig of beer in hopes the alcohol kicks in quick.

"Look," he says, leaning on the bar. "You didn't ask for advice—"

"Exactly."

His grin digs deeper. "But I'm gonna give it to ya anyway. Just don't fuck up and everything will be fine."

His words slice through the worry I've tried to keep stuffed. My gaze snaps to the bathroom to see her standing, arms over her chest, talking to Megan McCarter. I gulp. "I hope so, Peck. Damn it, I hope so."

"It's all in your hands, man. She's your girl. She knows it. You know it. I know it. Hell, Megan knows it and that's why she's over there trying to plant some seed of doubt in her brain."

"Megan wouldn't do that," I scoff. "There'd be no point. I've never fucked her or given her any idea that I even like her."

Peck's shoulders rise and fall. "I know y'all write off most of what I say, but I see a lot. You should listen to me."

"You see a lot and then you still have the hots for Molly McCarter?" I laugh. "We've all seen her ass, Peck."

His nose wrinkles as he grabs his beer. "Fuck you, Cross." He chuckles. "That's not the same."

I look back at Kallie again. She's heading our way with a furrowed brow. I toss her a smile and she returns it with enough reluctance it has me springing to my feet.

"Gonna check out the bulletin board," Peck says, clamping my shoulder as he walks by just as Kallie arrives.

"Hey," I say, holding out a hand. She takes it and gives it a gentle squeeze. "Everything all right?"

"Yeah." Lifting her glass filled with a pale yellow concoction, she downs a good three gulps. "And that's better."

"What's going on?"

"Not a thing. You ready to go?"

"Sure," I say, confused. "But is everything okay? I saw you talking to Megan and ..."

She squares up to me, her chin lifted. "You and Megan just work out together. Right?"

"Twice," I insist. "Once more and it's over. Why?"

"You've never had a thing for her?"

"Good, God, no." I laugh, pulling her into my chest. She's stiff for a moment before giving in and sinking into me. My face buries in her hair and I breathe her in, hoping it calms her as much as it does me to have her so close. "You're the only girl I've ever had a thing for." I pull away and kiss her forehead. "Ever."

"Forever ever?"

"Forever ever." I peer in her eyes. "I don't want to rush this thing between us, but I want you to know I have no desire, interest, or plans on being with anyone but you. Period."

"Forever ever?" She grins.

"Forever ever."

She takes our fingers, lacing them together, and pulls me toward the door.

"Is that going on your tab?" Machlan chuckles as we go by.

"That's my payment for all those things you could've moved by yourself the other day."

"I thought that was a favor?" He lifts a brow and looks to Kallie and smiles.

Laughing, I pop open the door and watch Kallie walk out. "It was. Thank you."

He winks.

Chapter 11

Kallie

"That glow says everything I need to know." Nora laughs, sitting down across from me at Carlson's.

"You don't know anything."

"Look me in the eye and tell me you haven't slept with Cross."

I grab a menu and hold it vertically between us in hopes of covering my blushed cheeks. It's not that there's anything to be embarrassed about, but it seems like it was so expected and I just caved.

How could I not?

I set myself up for this by going home from the golf course with him. It's absolutely what I wanted. But now the soreness between my legs is faded, a hint of concern is becoming evident.

Nora laughs from the other side. "So I was right. Go on, say it."

The menu drops to the table. "Of course you're right, but that squeal"—I point a finger in her direction—"is not necessary."

"Oh, yes it is! This is almost as good as Justin and Britney getting back together. It's the natural progression of things, the way they're supposed to be. How can I not celebrate this?"

"You realize you're essentially celebrating my orgasms, right?"

70

"Plural?" She throws her head back. "Of course plural. Fucking asshole." While I laugh at her reaction, she takes moment to recover. "So, I'm assuming he's better than before."

"He was always my best. No matter what, he was the bar I measured everyone else up to, you know? But now...it's like that's not the same person."

Nora's eyes grow wide as she gulps for effect.

"He's patient now, almost...tender? He kisses me and—"

"No more." Nora's hands are an inch away from her ears, mock trying to block out my recant of last night.

"What?" I giggle.

"I have to see him every Friday night at Crave. I don't want to be looking at him thinking of the way he kisses you in private time and all that. It would be weird."

Veronica comes out of nowhere and leans against the table. She pretends not to have overheard us for a minute and then, like the small-town business owner she is, she gives in. "You and Cross are together now, huh?"

"No," I say as Nora says, "Yes."

Veronica laughs. "I remember the two of you dating. You were always so cute, this big tough guy and a sweet little girl."

"Yeah, well, we aren't together," I say, looking at Nora pointedly. "We're feeling things out, I guess."

"I'd say you felt it out." Nora tosses me a wink. "You're fighting the universe here, Kal. You and Cross are supposed to be together, having beautiful little babies. You can't fight it forever."

"I'd say she's right. I saw how he was looking at you yesterday," Veronica chimes in. "But I'm glad to hear you aren't together right now, not officially, anyway." She looks down at her notepad and takes an ink pen out of her pocket like she just didn't say that.

Avoiding Nora's eyes and swallowing past the lump in my throat, I try to look unaffected. There's zero doubt she's toying with me, seeing if I'll take the bait she just dropped. I wish I could ignore it and continue on with my order and my day, but I'm not strong enough for that. "Why do you say that?"

"No big deal," she says, giving me a fake laugh. "He was just through the drive-through a few minutes ago with Megan, and we all know that girl's reputation."

"Cross was with Megan McCarter?" Nora asks. "Today?"

"Yeah. I mean, if he's not taken, how can you blame him? Men have needs," Veronica says.

"That's the biggest load of horse shit I've ever heard." Nora takes her menu and slams it into the condiments tray.

My hand visibly shakes as I try to get my menu lined up with hers. The plastic rattles as it swings back and forth, bouncing off the metal. Nora has sympathy and takes it from me then puts it away.

The lights of Crave twinkle overhead as I look into the eyes of the man I both love and hate.

"Did you sleep with her, Cross?"

His Adam's apple bobs. "No. I didn't sleep with her."

"Did you do anything with her? Because that's what they're saying," I gulp, my eyes stinging from the tears of the last few hours. They said he was with a redhead from Merom. All I knew is I couldn't find him. And now, here we are, and I almost wish I hadn't found him.

"We were at the same party," he admits.

"The one you weren't going to?"

"Come on, Kallie ..." He blows out a breath. The smell of alcohol is thick on his breath.

Blinking back another round of tears, I take a step back. "You come on," I tell him. "All you do is party. Drink. Be with God knows who."

"It's who I am," he says, his arms out to the side. He wobbles a little.

Walker stands a few feet away. I look at him.

"You drunk?" I ask, wiping my tears with the back of my hands.

"Nope," Walker replies.

"Good. He's all yours."

I didn't look back.

Maybe I shouldn't have now.

"I'm not with him," I say. It's aimed at Nora, my words directed across the table, but in reality, I'm saying it for me. "He is working with her at the gym."

"Look, I didn't mean to stir the pot..." Veronica looks at me with more smugness than I ever care to see on a person again. It sparks something inside me.

"No, you did." I slide out of my seat so we're eye-to-eye. "You always do."

"Kallie, really, I didn't."

"It's fine, Veronica," I tell her. "You know why? Because your small town gossip is all you have."

With a smile as deadly as I can make it, I swing myself in a half-circle and storm to the doors. Nora's voice trails behind me but I can't hear what she's saying. The white noise pulsing through my ears is too loud.

As soon as we're in Nora's car, I collapse into the soft leather seat. She flips on the engine but doesn't pull out.

"This is why I can't do this with him," I say out loud.

"Because Veronica is a bitch?"

"No, because this is what it always is." The words crack with emotion. "I don't want this and if I don't stop this shit with Cross, I'll be settling for a relationship I have to fight all the time."

"She could be lying, you know. Just saying."

"Yup." I yank my seatbelt down and click it in place. "That's why we're going to the gym."

"You sure?" she asks.

"Absolutely."

———

Cross

. . .

"Good workout today, Cobble. See ya next week." I grab a towel and wipe my face off as my fourth appointment of the day gathers his things. Usually by this time of day, my ass is dragging, but not today. Today I have so much damn energy I could train an entire football team.

A few minutes will go by and I'll forget I spent the night with Kallie. I'll get caught up in teaching a jab or timing a round on the jump rope and she'll momentarily be gone from my mind.

Then I'll remember.

The image of her spread out on my bed, how soft her skin felt last night as I held her tight against me will come charging back, and I immediately have another spark in my step.

It doesn't seem real in many ways. This girl I thought I lost, the girl I knew I'd never stop thinking about is all of a sudden back and has fallen in step with me again. I'm in all the way with Kallie.

Thank God.

The door chimes and I look up, expecting to see Cobble leaving. I do, but I also see Kallie walking in.

"Hey, babe..." My voice drifts off as I take in the look on her face. "What's wrong?"

"Nothing. Not really."

"Then why do you look like you lost your puppy?"

She crosses her arms and then drops them. She crosses them again. "How has your day been?"

"Good. Getting better—I think," I add, still unsure as to what's causing her to fidget with the hem of her shirt. "How was yours?"

"Fine." She heads to the free weights and drags her finger over them. "Did you train Megan today?"

"Yup. Last session. She took it reasonably well."

She raises a brow. "Took what?"

"The fact that I'm not training her anymore," I explain. "We talked about that. What did you think I meant?"

"That's why I'm here."

Her arms go across her middle again, this time firmly. She takes a deep breath, almost like she's counting to ten before blowing it out. It makes me take one too in an attempt to settle the little fire that starts to burn in my gut.

"So, the things you said to me last night, Cross, about how this changed things between us..."

"Yeah?"

"Exactly how did you mean that?"

"I meant it like if I see a man hitting on you, I'll break his face. Exact enough?" I'm partially teasing, but she there is no levity in her reaction. Instead, she bites the inside of her cheek.

"I was just in Carlson's with Nora. Veronica said you and Megan were in your truck—"

"Woah. Hold up." I throw the towel at the basket near the wall. "What the fuck is going on?"

"So, you were with her today? Getting lunch?"

"No—well, yes, I took her to Carlson's and grabbed a sandwich because it was the easiest fucking way to get her out of my hair."

Her jaw clenches as she huffs. "Really, Cross?"

"Yes, fucking really," I say back. My head spins in disbelief. "She had Molly drop her off here and she didn't come to pick her up. Was that intentional? Probably. Did I want it to happen? Absolutely not."

"Explain to me again why she was in your truck getting lunch?"

Forcing a swallow, I try to be calm. "I needed to head to the school for a boxing class I was putting on for the sophomore class. Megan was still here. What was I supposed to do? Leave her on the sidewalk?"

"That's where whores usually do their work. She'd probably feel right at home."

"When did you get so mean?" I laugh.

"When I feel messed with."

"Look, I was just trying to move on with my day. I wasn't fucking her. She wasn't blowing me. It was nothing like that."

She turns her back to me, looking at the parking lot. "I need to move on with my day too."

There's a finality in her tone, an insinuation that she doesn't just mean her day. Panic shoots through my veins and I'm to her before she can even take a step. "Hey, don't get crazy." My hands go to her hips. I feel her body wanting to cave back into mine, but she doesn't let it. "I'll cancel my last session today if you'll go home with me."

"I..." She gulps. "I have things to do today."

"You do not."

"Yeah, I do."

"Then come over tonight," I offer. There's a level of begging in my tone I'm not proud of, but can't deny.

"I'm helping Mom sort things she pulled out of the attic."

"Want me to help?" I ask, running my hands up and down her arms.

"No."

"Kallie," I groan, twisting her around. "Stop it."

"I think you're right. That's exactly what I'll do," she says, looking away from me. "At least for now."

"Oh, no. You're not doing this." I bite down the panic rising in my throat. "I won't let you do this."

She snorts, flipping her gaze to mine. It's steeled, with an iciness to it I haven't seen since that night way back when. "Me? What in the world am I doing, Cross?"

"You're not giving me the benefit of the doubt."

All I can see is her walking away from Crave that night years ago and feeling so hollow every minute of my life after. If she leaves again, I won't survive it. I can't re-invent myself again. I can't trick myself into hoping it'll all work out every morning when the sun comes up.

"No," she says with a simple shrug. "I'm not, because I've been through this with you before and I don't know why I thought it might be different this time. It's not."

"The hell it's not!" I roar, taking a step back. "I fucking love you, Kallie. I've waited on you to come back for years and you tell me it's not different? Maybe you're not different, but I fucking am!"

She blanches, stepping away from me too. The corners of her eyes wet as she takes another step back. "Maybe we both are."

My chest reverberates as I watch her take each step toward the door. With each inch of distance added between us, the air stagnates. A hollowness begins to form in my chest, and I know it will never fill this time.

"I love you," I tell her, my voice the softest this gym has ever heard.

"Do you? Do you really?" There's a fear in her eyes that chills me. "Or do you love what we were? Or what we could've been? Is it easier to settle for me because it's the easiest solution?"

Her words hit my heart like a poisoned dart. I take a step back. "You think I'm settling for you?"

"Maybe."

Forcing a swallow, I sigh. "You want to know something? I had this big thing worked up to tell you I loved you but then I thought it would be better to show you, to make you believe it so much you didn't have to ask or wonder," I admit. "Guess that failed."

"I need time to think," she says, her voice seeping with unshed tears. "I forgot what it's like to date in a small town. It's so damn hard."

"It's not hard if you love someone. You take the truth for the truth and the shit for what it is—shit." My head nods as I pick up a clean towel. "I've never, ever cheated on you, Kal. Have I messed up? Sure. Should I have had Megan in my truck? Maybe not, but I've been alone for a long time and I forgot about dating in a small town too."

"I hate this," she says. "I hated the rumors then and I hate them now. Sitting there with Veronica acting like I don't know some big secret is awful, Cross, and I've spent a lot of years in that position, whether you were really cheating on me or not. It hurts. It eats away at you."

"And being accused over and over eats away at me too." I wipe my face with the towel, scrubbing a little harder than necessary. "I can't make you love me any more than you could change who I was back then. I changed because I wanted to, but I can't make you love me if you don't want to."

Her tears fall. I want to go to her and hold her and kiss them away, but I don't. I leave her to them. She's the one who wants to believe a stupid-as-shit reason enough to warrant them falling.

The last time she cried in front of me, I didn't see her again. The reality of that pain rips through my chest and it's unbearable.

Before she can leave me again, I turn away from her and head into the back room.

Chapter 12

Cross

"I told you." Walker kicks back on the sofa in his living room with a look I'd like to knock off his face. While I'm ninety-five percent sure I could take him, the five percent isn't a risk I want to take tonight. "If they wanna go, let 'em go."

"This is such bullshit," I spit out, grabbing a beer off the coffee table. "I didn't do anything with Megan fucking McCarter. Not at any point in my life have I ever even touched her."

"I have." He grins. "But good choice not to—it's not worth it."

Every inch of my skin itches. It's uncomfortable, making me feel like I need to move, to run, to rip something to shreds.

"I'm caught between a rock and a hard place," I comment, more to the universe as a whole rather than to Walker specifically. "As pissed as I am right now, I know she's the girl I was meant to have. If I don't go after her, I'll lose her, but if I do, doesn't that make me look guilty? Or like a pussy? Or set the stage for a power vacuum in our relationship?"

"Yeah."

"Yeah? That's all you got?"

He turns off the football game and sighs. "Look, man, I'm not the best guy to go to for relationship advice...obviously."

"You're all I fucking have right now."

"Oh, so I was the last resort?"

"No, Lance was the last resort. You are whatever falls before that."

Walker laughs. "You're not as dumb as I thought you were."

"Here's the difference between my situation and yours," I tell him, bending forward and resting my elbows on my knees. "You didn't care. I love her."

"Love is such an overrated thing, Cross. What's it really mean, anyway? How long does it last? Who the fuck knows. I'm with Sienna not because I love her, although I do, I'm sure, but because there's no other option I can live with. Period. There are too many variables to make decisions based on love."

"Maybe I don't know what it is."

"Know what what is?" Peck asks as he rounds the corner. "By the way, the alternator is changed on the SUV in the shop."

"Do you knock?" Walker asks. "But good work on the SUV."

"No, and thanks. Now, what are we talking about? You look so serious."

I take a minute to fill Peck in, getting more irritated as I go. Before I'm finished, I see he's side-eyeing Walker.

"First of all, whatever that jackass has told you, ignore it—all of it," Peck says.

Walker shrugs. "He asked."

"Second of all, you need to head that way now and apologize."

"Me?" I bark. "I didn't do anything."

"And do you really want the rest of your life messed up because you were so worried about your ego that you wouldn't apologize?"

I snort. "It's not ego. It's principle."

"You can call it whatever you want, it's the same damn thing. Either you want to feel like you have some high and mighty set of principles, which we all know you don't, or you can get the girl—your pick. I'd pick her, because she's really hot."

Narrowing my eyes, I watch Peck laugh.

"Nah, not really because she's hot, because she's nice. She's sweet. She gave you a second chance," he throws in. When I don't react, he stands. "Do what you want, but don't come a-cryin' to me when she's at the bar with someone else."

"I'll kill them," I snarl.

"Then avoid prison and go apologize."

He tells Walker something about a transmission, but I can't hear it over the roar of blood over my ears. Walker turns the television back on, but I can't figure out who has the ball or what the score is because I'm mulling over Peck's advice.

The thought of going home and never having her in my kitchen, in my bed, on my sofa again twists me up so bad I don't even want to go. My phone sits in my pocket, and its failure to ring or buzz with a call or text from her hurts my heart.

I sit for a few more long minutes before I just can't sit any longer. "I'm gonna go," I tell Walker, standing. "May as well get a workout in since all I want to do is hit something."

Walker doesn't even look up. "Tell Kallie I said hi."

Chapter 13

Kallie

The bags crunch as they hit the countertop, and Mom starts sorting through the groceries. She doesn't even have to look at me to know something is wrong.

"Are you going to tell me or do you want me to guess?" she asks.

Curled up on a kitchen chair, my hair in a messy bun, I sniffle. "I don't want to talk about it."

"If you didn't want to talk about it, you would be in your bedroom or driving around a back road, not sitting in the kitchen."

Putting my feet on the floor, I straighten my shirt. I don't know how to talk about this with my mother. She loves Cross maybe as much as she loves me, and I'm not sure her opinion will be unbiased. Yet, she's my mom. I just need my mom.

"Did you date Daddy in a small town?" I ask.

Her hand stills in the air before she puts the jar of peanut butter in the cabinet. "We dated in Detroit, mostly. We were newlyweds when we moved down here. Why do you ask?"

"Nora and I went into Carlson's today and Veronica told me Cross had a woman in his car today, buying lunch."

"I see." She turns around and leans against the counter. "Did you ask him if it was true?"

"Yes, and he admitted it."

"He did?" she asks, surprised.

"He said she wouldn't leave the gym and he had somewhere to be," I say, testing the words out loud for the first time since I calmed down.

"Do you believe that?"

"Megan is that way, but he shouldn't have had her in his truck."

She takes a deep breath before turning back to her groceries. "I'm a little bit in shock."

"Me too." I sigh. "I hate this, Mom. I hate the way everyone gossips and almost sets you up to be a joke."

"No one made a joke out of you." She spins on her heel. "She made a tramp out of herself, but that's the end of that."

A flood of warmth trickles through my body as I watch my mother watch me. Just knowing she has my back and is in my corner helps—a lot.

"I left here because he wouldn't grow up and I was sick of the gossip," I remind her. "Then my ex in Indiana cheated on me, and now I'm back and it's the same damn thing. Senseless drama. I hate it."

"Then don't buy into it, honey."

"I don't! I just want a love like in the movies. Is that too much to ask?"

"Movies are drama. Just pointing that out," she says.

I roll my eyes. "I want the happy. The trust. The breakfast in bed and the flowers at work. I want that, Mom. Not all ... this."

She sticks a gallon of milk in the fridge, pausing. "Maybe what you're seeing is how the world really works, Kal. I know you see pictures and movies of perfect little houses and marriages and friendships, but it's not real. None of it. Real comes raw with other people's influences and you can't get out of that. It's unavoidable. Life is a bitch."

"Don't I know it."

"The key to happy relationships is trust. It's the hardest thing to master, but if you can, it's the secret key that opens a world you can never know otherwise."

"But doesn't trusting someone leave you exposed? They can stick a knife in you and twist it." I wince, thinking that's exactly how I felt this afternoon.

"Yeah, it does. It leaves you wide open, but you can't get through that door without doing it. You just have to learn who you can trust and who you can't."

"So, basically, conquer Rome in a day? Got it." Wiping the fog off my glass of ice water, I think back to Cross's face. "He was mad at *me*, Mom. Can you believe that?"

"I'd be more worried if he wasn't."

"Why?"

A soft smile ghosts across her lips. "Maybe it insulted him that you would accuse him of something. Maybe he thought you knew him better than that."

"It still doesn't make this any easier."

"The world isn't black and white. It's a wonderful mixture of the two that has a lot of blurry lines, and if you care what people do and say, you have a long life ahead of you, honey." She sits across from me and folds her hands on the table. "Trust your gut, and remember what led you back to him in the first place."

She gets up, kisses me on the head, and walks down the hallway. Her words, however, stay behind.

———

Kallie

The dog across the street barks, breaking the late-night silence. My car starts up, the lights shining into the living room as I back down the driveway.

My stomach is all twisted, an ulcer beginning to form somewhere in the pit of my bowels. No matter what I do—read, sing, or create—I can't stop thinking about Cross.

Walking five miles just got me a sore hamstring, doing the dishes left me with a sliced finger, and I've sung the hell out of my favorite playlist on my phone. Through it all, I've thought about him.

It's those first nights in Indiana all over again. It's the emptiness in my soul, the craving to love and be loved...by him, only him. It's only ever been him.

My ex-boyfriend didn't help that. Maybe he distracted me for a bit, but the hole in my heart just started to fill recently.

The car glides down the street, heading into town, the streetlights getting more frequent as I go. The clock reads almost one in the morning, and my body shivers against the cool summer night.

A peace settles over me as I drive. I'm more confident in this decision than I've ever been. It's right. I've never felt stronger about something, not even when I left him the first time. I'm not the same person as I was then. Neither is he. Why would I think we'd be the same as we were then now?

Screw the rumors.

Fuck the gossips.

To Hell with being unsure.

Life is a risk and, at the end of the day, his love is the surest bet I can make. It's at least worth a shot.

A set of headlights comes my way and the driver clicks them down, turning off the brights. As we pass, I glance over my shoulder and see Cross's face.

My heart leaps in my chest as his tail lights come on in the rear view, his tires squealing as he rips the truck around. Before I know what's happening, he's behind me, traveling in the same direction.

The high school is a block ahead and I turn my turn signal on in hopes he'll slow down a bit and get off my ass. My throat is constricted as I pull in, my blood pounding in my veins as I stop the car. He's out of his truck and around the front before I ever even get the door open. He does the honors for me.

His hair is wild, his shirt soaked with sweat. "You okay?"

My feet on the asphalt, I stand and breathe him in. "I was coming to look for you."

"I'm sorry."

"Nope," I say, shaking my head.

"Dammit, Kal—"

I take the words out of his mouth with my own, pressing my lips against his so quickly it shocks him. My hands go to his damp hair, urging him to kiss me harder. I need this. I need...him.

He finally pulls away, dragging in a lungful of air. "Kallie?"

"*I am sorry*," I say, resting my forehead on his.

"It was me that had her in my truck."

"And it was my insecurities that let that matter. I mean, yeah, don't do it again"—I laugh—"but you didn't exactly do something wrong."

"It was wrong if it makes you feel anything but great." He wraps me up in his arms, pulling me to his chest. "I was at the gym, working out, and all I could see was you standing there mad at me."

"I was sitting on my bed and kept thinking about how last night I was in yours, how many nights I wished to be there, and how tonight I wasn't because I was mad, like a child."

He squeezes me tighter. "I was also wrong when I said I couldn't make you love me. I damn sure am going to try for the rest of my life."

My hand stills on his back, his heartbeat picking up against my cheek. "If there's one thing I know, it's that being with you, at least trying it again, isn't settling for anything other than the possibility of ... everything I've ever wanted."

My words cause his heart to rapid-fire and I pull away. "Cross?"

"I want to marry you," he whispers under the lights of the parking lot. "But I want to ask your mother before I ask you, and I want to find the perfect ring and the perfect spot first. You deserve that."

"I don't need any of that," I say, choking back a sob. I'm so desperate for him, my chest coming undone and overflowing. "I just need you. I'm never letting you go again."

"Damn right you're not." His body shakes with his chuckle. "Do you want to ride with me back to my house or have me follow you?"

Grinning through my tears, I pull away and look into his spectacular green eyes. "Follow me."

"The view of your behind is one of my favorites."

I swat at his arm, but he pulls me in for a quick kiss instead.

"Hey, Cross?"

"Yeah?"

I grab his hand and lace our fingers together. "I love you."

"I love you too."

Epilogue

C ross
  A few weeks later

"Why does golf always end up with fucking? Not that I'm complaining." He grins, looking at me over his shoulder.

The streetlights create shadows in the cab of his truck as we make our way back to his house after a night of fun. We watched a chick flick that he hated, ate seafood that I hated, then capped it off with four holes of putt-putt before we turned our sticks in and parked on the first desolate back road we found so we could have sex.

"I guess you like the way I handle balls," I suggest, making him laugh. "Really? I don't know. It's weird though."

"I guess it's not that different from anything else we do. Dinner?"

"Fucking."

"Laundry?"

"Oh, I love when we do it on spin cycle," I note.

"Painting the back porch?"

"Yeah, but sex in public isn't my thing. You caught me on a bad day." I giggle.

"First of all, it's not public. Second, I was thinking it was a really, really good day."

Grinning, I blow out a breath and settle into the seat.

Being in Linton has changed everything for me—finding Cross again, reconnecting with my mother, finding a career in a firm that's a lot quieter, but more fulfilling.

When I was younger, all I wanted was to get out of my hometown. Everything here was full of drama and complications and distractions. Even now, it's not without its faults. That's for sure. I still deal with the whispers of women who want Cross, still hear murmurings at the soda fountain at Goodman's while I get my daily drink, but now that I'm older and maybe a little wiser, none of that matters. All that matters is the way he looks at me.

"Crave is up ahead. Want to go in for a while?" Cross asks. "Machlan wanted to talk to me about expanding his business. I thought it might be a good investment."

"Sure, but do you think you can talk to him on a Friday night? Crave is always so busy."

"If not, at least we'll be entertained. I'm sure something is going on in there. Peck will be there. That's promising enough."

I laugh.

He pulls the truck over to the side of the street. We climb out and he grabs my hand like he always does but stops and starts digging around in his pocket. Pulling out his phone, he furrows his brow and drops my hand.

"Fucking great," he mutters, shoving the device back in his pocket.

"What was that all about?" I say, taking his hand again.

"Hadley is coming home."

"Don't look so happy about it," I laugh as we head towards the bar. "Don't you want to see your sister?"

"Yup. I just don't want to do it here."

"And why not?"

He nods towards the building. "Machlan. Hadley comes and it becomes a war around here and I'm in the middle of it. They subscribe to some hate love bullshit. They need to pick a side and go."

"Could be fun," I tease. "Imagine the hate sex."

"I could never hate you. But," he says, grabbing my ass, "I could subscribe to that too for a while if that's what you want."

"Too? What else you subscribing to over there, Cross?" I laugh.

He stops and stands in front of me. His green eyes look like slices of pure jade in the hazy streetlights. "I subscribe to one theory, and one theory only."

"What's that?"

"To keep you wanting to be my girl."

"Always."

The End

Crash: A Gibson Boy Short Story

A Gibson Boy Short Story

Chapter One

Nora

"I think I've learned more in the last half hour than I've learned in my entire life." Machlan leans against the cooler, his large, muscled arms crossed over his chest.

"Go with us tonight and I'll teach you some more." My friend Emily leans forward, her boobs resting on the bar. She flashes my boss, and one of my best friends, the sexiest smile she can muster.

"He's not the lamb he's pretending to be," I warn. "From the stories I hear, he could teach even you a thing or two, Em."

She laughs, her eyes shining. "That's what I'm counting on."

Holding Machlan's gaze, she licks her lips with the deliberateness of a seasoned vet. My group of friends burst into laughter. Me? I just shake my head. This is simply a variation of every woman's reaction to Machlan Gibson.

I get it. I do. He checks off every box on the "what makes a man hot" list. Even though he's practically a brother to me at this point, I can still see it. I don't want it, or want to see it, but I see it.

"How many panties were thrown behind the bar tonight?" I ask, demonstrating my point. "I found a pink one and a red one."

"Women really do that?" Emily asks. "I thought that was just something from movies."

"Oh, they do that." I laugh, wiping down the bar. "Sometimes worse. And the notes women leave him on the bulletin board by the door are downright disgusting."

Machlan shrugs. "I can't help it. Being this good-looking is a liability."

"Shut up." The laugh I'm trying to hold back surfaces, causing my friends to giggle again. "And you two aren't helping," I say, pointing at them.

"What can I say?" Emily asks. "Hot bartenders are my thing. My guilty pleasure."

"I thought penises were your guilty pleasure." Lauren laughs.

Emily shrugs. "I do like a good penis. I'll admit that."

"Who doesn't?" I sigh, thinking of my last romp with a well-endowed man.

It's been too long for me. It's not that I'm promiscuous, exactly. I'm choosy about who I'm with and I don't sleep around a lot. I have a few men, a handful, maybe that I can count on for a good time on a rainy Saturday night. But lately they've all been lackluster ... all except the one I wish was so I could quit thinking about him.

"Um, I don't like a good penis." Machlan shoves off the cooler, sticking his hands in his pockets. He looks at me, lifting a brow.

I know what he's doing before he does it because he does it to me all the time. He puts me on the spot. Tests me—for what, I don't know. It's like he's toying with me to see if he can get me to crack. It could be because I don't react to him like every other breathing female does. Whatever it is, I hold my breath and prepare to not, in fact, crack.

"So, Nora," he says, leaning against the bar. "What's your guilty pleasure?"

"Probably something lame compared to yours." I lean forward too, mocking his stance. He's on one end of the bar, me on the other, with my friends in the middle. "Why don't you share yours with the class?"

"That's what I was thinking." Emily grins.

Machlan looks at her with a wide, cheesy smile before turning his attention to Lauren. "You're up. What's your guilty pleasure?"

"Well," my soft-spoken friend says, "I'm married with a baby, so can I say showering alone?"

"No one should ever shower alone," Machlan teases.

"Trust me. When you have kids, things like showering and peeing with the door closed is the guiltiest of pleasures," Lauren sighs.

"That's so, so sad," I lament. "And also, why I'm not sure I ever want kids. I don't want to give up ... *me*."

Lauren's eyes sparkle, partially from the lemon drop martini she downed like a camel and partially from thoughts of her baby girl. "It's so worth it. Every hour of no sleep. Every night with screams of colic. Every poop bomb that goes up their back—"

"No kids." Machlan laughs. "I'm getting on that train."

"Speaking of pulling trains ..." Emily says, her eyes pinned on the back of the room.

Peck strolls in, an Illinois Legends cap stuck backwards on his head. Blond, unruly locks peek out from under as he makes his way toward us.

Machlan takes all but three seconds to stand upright. "What's wrong?"

"Nothin'," Peck says, stopping at the head of the bar.

"And who are you?" Emily says, unconcerned with the look being exchanged between Machlan and Peck. "You look like a great time, baby."

"Em, hush a second," I say, waving her off. My heartbeat strums a little too quick, causing my lips to part to catch more air. With this guy, anything is possible. His heart is pure gold, but his actions aren't always logical. "What did you do, Peck?"

"I didn't do anything." He squishes his face together. "Not really. Just if anyone asks, I've been here since eleven."

"Seriously," I tell him. "Is this better or worse than the time you got thrown out of the skating rink?"

"I was fifteen," Peck deadpans. "But this is better. Or worse." He side-eyes Machlan. "Bob Shaw's tractor might be sitting in the middle of the road out by the water tower."

My head falls back as Machlan groans.

"I didn't do anything but borrow it," Peck insists. "I was going to bring it back. I just kind of ran it out of gas."

"Did Bob give you the keys? Say, 'here, Peck. Borrow my tractor at midnight'?"

When Peck doesn't respond, Machlan punches him in the arm.

"Um, Nora?" Lauren asks. "Is everything okay?"

"Everything is great," Peck says, brushing off Machlan. "What were we talking about?"

"Guilty pleasures," Emily chimes in. "Have one?"

Peck's boyish grin gets a sigh from Lauren. As dark and outright sexy as Machlan is, his cousin is the opposite. Tall, thin, with baby blue eyes, Peck's attractiveness stems from his charm. He's kind and sweet and a little goofy—totally Lauren's speed if she weren't married.

As I look at Emily, it might be her speed too.

"Back off, Em. You'd kill him." I laugh.

Peck scoffs, his lips pressed together to bite back a grin. "You underestimate me, Nora."

"Oh, do I?"

"You most certainly do." He folds his hands in front of him, leaning on the bar. His Nirvana t-shirt is a little washed out and smells like the outdoors as he moves. "My guilty pleasure, huh? I like s'mores."

"S'mores?" Emily grins. "I can get with that."

"I'm starting to think you can get with whatever comes through the door," Machlan jabs.

"You judging?" she asks.

Machlan shakes his head, turning his attention to me. "Where do you find these girls?"

"She actually found me in the bathroom of Court Pub over in Lancaster," Emily groans. "Long story. Bad night."

"Great story. Entertaining night," I offer. "I guess we see it a little differently."

"I didn't look good with no pants to put on. It doesn't matter how you look at it." Emily gives me a pointed look then promptly affixes her attention on Machlan. "I actually look great with no pants, if you were wondering. Just not that particular moment in time. I can prove it."

Machlan laughs, his cheeks turning a soft shade of pink. "I gotta get out of here, Nora. Can you finish up?"

"Sure. I just have to check the register and I think it's good to go. I can lock up ..."

My voice trails as a sound raps on the door. Machlan and I glance at each other. This is why he doesn't let me stay alone at night, afraid someone will pop in late and try to rob me. It's never happened and I can't see it happening in Linton, but it's a hard and fast rule of my boss. Either he stays or Peck stays, sometimes even his friend Cross comes by to walk me to my car. It's sweet, predictable Gibson boy behavior.

"Stay put," Machlan says, rounding the corner.

We sit quietly as Machlan peeks out of the blinds next to the door. He pulls away, his eyes lit up. "It's Kip," he whispers.

"Ah," I moan as Peck's eyes grow wide.

"Shit," he says. "Remember: eleven o'clock. I was here from eleven until about ... half hour ago."

"Hang on, Kip," Machlan says, hiding his laugh. "Door is stuck."

The knock continues along with muffled threats from the other side. Machlan, ignoring everything Kip is telling him, waves a hand at Peck to follow him. "Let's go."

"Isn't that aiding and abetting?" Lauren asks.

"Yup. And it's gonna be so much fun." Machlan cackles. "Nora, cover for us."

My friends look at me in amazement as I shake my head, watching the two boys leave through the back. My attention is turned back to the door when Kip pounds on it again.

"Girls," I say, looking at Lauren and Emily, "you're about to meet my guilty pleasure."

The door lock unfastens easily, the cool night air blowing in. Standing in the doorway in his brown uniform smelling of spice. He gazes down at me with his deep, dark brown eyes and lifts a brow.

"What can I do for you, Officer?" I ask, leaning against the doorframe.

My friends giggle from behind me, but Kip doesn't seem to notice. His gaze is leaving a trail of flames over my face, down my chest, across my stomach that's clenched at the site of him, and rolls over the apex of my things.

"Now or later?" he asks.

"Do I get a choice?"

The corner of his lip upturns, his gaze settling over my shoulder. "Business first, darlin'. Is Peck here?"

"Nope."

His eyes dart back to mine. "I know he's here because his truck is out back."

"Well, he was but left about thirty minutes ago." I shrug.

"Did he leave with Machlan?"

"I have no idea." I smirk.

"Nora!" Lauren hisses. "You can't lie to an officer."

Kip grins, the gesture soaking my panties. He works his chiseled jaw back and forth, his eyes narrowing. "She's right. You can't."

"I think you can't do lots of things with a police officer that I've done. Seems very tit for tat, doesn't it, Kip?"

He takes a step toward me but stops when Emily speaks.

"Do you guys need some alone time?"

My stomach twists into a tight knot as Kip licks his lips.

"Yes, ladies. If you don't mind. I need to speak to Nora in private," he says, his eyes never leaving mine. "I believe she has information she's withholding."

"I bet you do," Emily teases.

The sound of them gathering their things and their heels clicking against the floor doesn't register. All I can hear is the slight uptake of breath from the beautiful man in front of me. All I can feel are his eyes slowly undressing me in the doorway. All I can taste is the sweetness of his lips that haven't touched mine. Yet. But they will. They always do.

Thank God.

Chapter Two

Nora

Emily slides into the passenger's seat of Lauren's car seconds before Lauren pulls out onto the road with a promise to not fall asleep until I get there. That's all fine and good. I hope it's a very long, wet time before I show up to Emily's house.

Kip takes a step, the another, toward me. I back into the heated bar, the door snapping closed behind us.

"Well, Nora," he says, his boots heavy on the floor. "What do you have to say for yourself?"

"I'm wet?" I offer, leaning against the bar. "My pussy throbs? Does that suffice?"

His grin darkens, his eyelids growing heavy. "I'd say it's a good start."

"You want more detail?"

"Always," he growls. He stands so he's in between my legs, the fabric of his pants rubbing against the tender skin of my legs. "Why didn't you answer my calls this week?"

"I was busy," I tease.

"Too busy to return a fucking call?"

"Well, if I knew the call was about fucking, I might've answered."

"Is it ever about anything else?"

Grabbing the lapels of his shirt, I jerk him toward me. "It better not be or I'll never answer it again."

His lips crash against mine before I get the last syllable out. He breathes in the words, captures them with his mouth. My hands are in his hair, working the silky strands between my fingers as our kisses grow deeper.

Our tongues dance as his hands grasp my ass, fingers digging into the denim covering my bottom. He lifts me up, sitting me on a barstool, never breaking the kiss.

My head spins like it does every time we hook up because that's just what it is—a hookup. That's also why it's amazing. I can enjoy myself, be myself, and then be myself with someone else tomorrow if I want to. It doesn't matter.

"I've dreamed of this fucking ass," he growls in my mouth.

"You've dreamed," I pant, "of this fucking ass or fucking this ass?"

"The first but I'll happily take the second." He buries his head in the side of my neck, kissing and biting his way to the hollow of my throat. "Is Machlan here?"

"Nope. He's with Pec ... He's not here."

He pulls back as I make a face, catching my slip-up.

"I know he's with Peck and I know they left when I got here. I'm not fucking stupid."

My legs swinging off the barstool, I grin. "Apparently you are because I still have clothes on." Hopping off the stool, pressing a palm against his chest, I look up at him. "Guess I'll finish closing."

"The hell you will."

He lifts the hem of my shirt up and over my head before I realize what he's doing. The air, combined with Kip's hooded eyes, peaking my nipples. The ends of my hair brush against my bare shoulders as he makes quick work of my pants. I assist by sliding out of my shoes and socks and kicking everything to the side.

"Like what you see?" I ask, taking my breasts out of the bra and letting them sit on top. "Because if you do, and by the strain of your pants right now—I think you do, you better lose some clothes, Kip."

He flips me a look, but frees the buttons dotting the center of his chest. "I hate how bossy you are."

"I think you really like it," I tell him. Closing the distance between us, I undo his belt. "I need you inside me. You're taking too long."

"You could've told me Peck was in the back and I could've tossed those friends of yours outta here earlier. I could've been buried in that sweet little pussy by now."

My thighs clench, my stomach aching with the need to feel his cock part me in two. My hands fumble with the button on his pants. All I can think of is the release he's about to give me.

"Here," he says, working faster. "Let me help."

His pants are pooled at his feet around his work boots, his body otherwise on full display. Shoulders, as broad as the room, cut narrowly to a trim, fit waist. You can tell he runs by the leanness of his body, but he fills out just the right parts to keep from looking too thin.

He's glorious. The little scars and wounds speckling his torso and thighs adding that much more mystery to a man I don't ever want to solve. It's the mystery that keeps this fun. Sexy. Exciting. If that dissolves, he'll just be like every other guy on a Friday night. And, as I look down, I'm reminded just how much he's not like every other guy.

His cock is pointed to the ceiling, a dot of pre-cum catching the light. He's so hard, so thick, so perfectly sized to stretch me open and fill me up.

"Wait," I say, wrapping my hand around the base. My tongue hits the salty liquid, smearing it over the head before I suck him inside my mouth. The rawness in his groan, the way his hands sink in my hair as he thrusts forward and rocks himself into my mouth, has my entire body screaming for him.

"You know what I hate about this?" he rasps.

"Hmm," I hum, flicking the tip with my tongue. I pump his length, swollen and veiny, as I suck him in and out.

"That I'm on duty. I gotta make this quick, sweetheart."

"Ew," I say, standing up. "Don't call me that."

He rolls on the condom, grinning. "I forgot. Nothing feel-y."

"Nothing remotely feel-y, please. You're my guilty pleasure."

There's a sparkle shining in his eye that should warn me, but I'm too high on pheromones to read it correctly. He reaches into the heap of clothes at his feet and brings up a set of handcuffs. "If you're guilty, then I'm gonna have to cuff you, Miss."

"Oh, no," I say as sweetly as I can. "Please no. I'm a good girl." Batting my lashes, I resist the urge to giggle. Holding my hands out, palms up, I pout. "What will I ever do with cuffs on?"

He slaps them against my wrists, the cold metal biting my wrists. It sends a wave of fire through my core, landing at the apex of my thighs.

I can feel my heartbeat in my pussy, my legs feeling like I've ran a marathon as they fill with adrenaline. The sound of the metal zipping as he latches the cuffs on tighter, making the bite sting even more, has me almost moaning.

"I'll tell you what you're gonna do," he whispers. Holding my gaze, he drops to his knees in front of me. "You're going to stand still and not shout, okay?"

"When am I ever quiet?" I say, breaking character. "I mean, I'll try, Officer."

A hand slides between my legs and urges them apart. One hand cupping each side of my groin, his thumbs perilously close to my ass, he buries his face between my legs. My hands bound together, I bring them over his head and pull him toward me.

He inhales roughly, breathing in the scent of my arousal. His hands shake, betraying the cool confidence he tries to portray.

"Lean back," he orders as he rocks back on his heels. Checking to ensure the bar is behind me, I do as I'm told.

His thumbs part my slit. The contact alone, of his hands on my delicate flesh, sends ripples of excitement through my veins.

"I lied to you." He moves the pad of one finger over my clit. I have no idea what he's going to say and lying is a hard limit for me, right along with feels, but I don't care. All I can do is melt under his touch. "I said this was going to be quick."

"Keep rubbing me like that and it will be quick." I moan, tilting my hips toward him.

Contact breaks. "Better stop then."

"Kip," I warn, my eyes flying open, "I swear to you, if you don't—ah!"

His mouth is on me, sucking in my swollen bud. It's a shot of ecstasy straight to my blood.

"Fuck you," I barely get out, my brain-mouth connection fraying. "Don't. Stop."

His tongue is thick and heavy, working its way around my body like a backroad. One finger slips inside me, giving me a taste of what's to come.

"Still," he growls. The vibrations of his voice against me makes me shudder. It also makes me *not* still, much to his frustration. One hand flat against my stomach, one wrapped around my backside, he holds me tight. "Still, Nora."

"The fact I can still talk makes you not quite as effective as you want to—damn you!"

Two fingers are inserted, taking away my breath. I rock myself onto them, needing the friction. Dying for the friction. Craving the friction.

"You are so fucking gorgeous when you're like this," he says, the need in his voice undeniable.

"Like what?" I grumble, irritated at the slow in tempo.

"On the cusp of getting off. It's fucking awesome."

Glancing down at this man on his knees in front of me, I grin.

"You know what's awesome? And don't stop that motion while you talk," I warn, swirling my hips against him.

"What's that?"

"Seeing your face with my juices all over it."

This sparks something inside him. His eyes darken to a shade I've only seen a couple of times before. His hand falls away from my body as he stands.

"Fuck you," he says, echoing my earlier sentiment.

"Please do."

He grins but catches himself. Instead, he takes my cuffed hands and guides me to a table. He sits on a chair and turns me away from him.

I glance over my shoulder to see him sitting, legs apart, cock in hand. It's struggling against the rubber of the condom, bulging for me.

"Let me sit down on you," I almost beg.

"I might."

"Dude, what if you—"

He stops me with a glare. "Don't call me dude."

"Fine, Officer," I hiss. "What if someone is dying and they call you out? Want to deal with that with blue balls?"

"I'm about tired of your bossiness."

"Fine," I say, starting to turn around. "I'll get someone else to get me off."

I'm jerked back around, my blood pressure spiking, as he grips both hips with his hands. He lowers me onto his cock inch-by-delicious-inch. Each movement filling me until the head is slammed against the back of my pussy.

"That," I breathe. The feeling of him at the wall is my kryptonite. It's the place not all men can hit but Kip can every fucking time. It's almost irritating how perfectly he can do that, but I'm not in a place to complain.

My body sags at the pressure building inside me. He doesn't move, doesn't thrust, just leaves himself seated deep inside my body.

I lean back against his hard chest, his hands coming around and cupping my breasts. He plays with my nipples, twisting them between his fingers, as he presses kisses up and down my shoulder.

"Kip ..." My voice trails off as I succumb to the moment. I don't have to think like this. There's nothing to worry about, nothing to consider. Just enjoying myself with a man that wants me, flaws and all.

"I'm going to tell you a secret," he whispers against my neck.

His lips touch the area right behind my ear, the place that leaves me breathless every time. There's something about that gesture that I love.

"This is your real guilty pleasure," he breathes.

"What?" I try to sit up, but he clamps me down against him. "You like this. As much as you want to pretend you're a little badass that doesn't want a connection, it's the connection that you really crave."

My head spins at his accusation. My body stills against him.

"You're wrong," I say, my voice without the strength I usually have.

"Fine." He chuckles, shoving his hips up. "You want to be fucked hard? You got it."

Chapter Three

N ora

Red rings circle my wrists. They're dangled in front of me while Kip, now fully clothed, unlocks them. It's immediate relief to have them gone, like a signal that snaps me back to reality.

"There you go," Kip says, tucking the cuffs back in the pocket on his belt. "I hope that was impersonal enough for you."

"It'll suffice." I wink. Turning around to gather my clothes, I get them on as quickly as possible. "I hate it when you get dressed first and make me wait."

"That's not my problem," he says, getting himself straightened out. "Who knows when I'll see that body again? I have to take it while I can get it."

Pivoting, I look at the flamingo lights decorating the wall behind the bar while I slip on my shoes. I don't want him to see the pink in my face, even though I could blame it on the three orgasms he just delivered with the quality of a professional.

107

"What's on your agenda tonight?" I ask, opting for small talk over any awkward silence ... or over against any unwanted segues into anything resembling serious discussions.

"I think Machlan and Peck headed over to Crank, so I'll drop by there before clocking out."

"You aren't going to do anything to Peck, are you?"

Kip chuckles. "Hell, no. Knowing him, he'll be over by Shaw's in the morning to apologize and will help on the farm out there all of next week even though old man Shaw will tell him not to worry about it."

Fully dressed and pinked-cheeks gone, I suck in a breath and turn around again. "Then why did you come by here all 'Where's Peck?' if you weren't going to do anything to him?"

He shrugs. "He's fun to fuck with. Besides, it looks good if I'm asked that I followed up with the report of an abandoned tractor. I wasn't even sure Peck did it until he jetted out of here."

"Oh my God." I laugh. "He's gonna kill you."

"Not if he doesn't find out."

He saunters toward me, closing the distance wickedly slow. Each step notches up the heat in my core again.

"It was nice seeing you tonight," he says. His tone is soft, yet rough, and it's what I'll reply over and over tonight as I hang out with my friends. It's also the one I need to stop focusing on.

"Nice seeing you too."

It's simple and clear. Concise. To the point. Not full of any vulnerability or emotion.

Kip smirks. "We're back to this, huh?"

"What are you talking about?" I scoff. "We never leave this."

"How long do we have to go fucking in closed bars, on bales of hay in the middle of farms, or against ladders leading up to the water tower before you realize you like me? Huh?"

"I like ya, Kip," I say grinning. "I like ya a lot. That's why I let you keep fucking me."

My heart hurts to say it because it's not completely true. I could like him, maybe even in the way I think he likes me. If I thought he believed my dismissal, even for a second, I'd probably say something sweet. Thank God, he doesn't.

"Lucky me." He laughs. He presses a kiss to my cheek. "At least your consistent."

"I appreciate consistency."

He rolls his eyes, grabbing a walkie-talkie from the bar. "Fine. Be a hard-ass. Call me when you want more dick."

"Will do. It was a pleasure doing business with you."

I don't get to see his face to study his reaction, but the little snort that drifts behind him as he turns toward the door makes me smile. His hand is on the knob, his back to me, when he stops.

"Hey, Nora?"

"Yeah?"

"My guilty pleasure is smart-mouthed bartenders with eyes the color of the water in movies and that smell like the flowers that used to grow behind my mom's house." He glances at me with those big, broody eyes. "See ya."

THE END

If you've read the complete Gibson Boys Series—don't forget about Blaire! Her story, RESTRAINT, is out now! Read it on Amazon.

Restraint
MASON FAMILY SERIES
USA Today Bestselling Author
ADRIANA LOCKE

Acknowledgments

First, as always, thank God for the blessings in my life and the ability to do what I love.

I'd also like to thank Mr. Locke for his unwavering support and to the Little Locke's for their enthusiasm as I finish a book. I love you all so very much.

Thanks, too, to my mama, Aunt Judy, Peggy, and Rob for their love and understanding as to why I'm always busy. Also, thanks for telling *all* of your friends about my books. Ha!

Massive hugs to Kari March for making another gorgeous cover. Becca with Evident Ink and Marla Esposito both worked on edits for this project at one time or another—thank you! Also thanks to Kylie and the Team at Give Me Books for rocking, per usual.

A huge shout out to Tiffany, my PA, for keeping me in line. Kisses to Mandi Beck for being the best friend ever. Hugs to Jen and Susan for never giving up on me, and to Carleen for being the yin to my yang. Thank you also to Candace that doesn't let me forget I need to write every day.

High-fives to the Team Player girls. That was a once-in-a-lifetime experience. Or was it?

Thanks to Kaitie, Jade, Stephanie, and Ebbie for managing parts of my groups. You are the best!

Thanks to Jess Fadden for testing everything I think I'm screwing up. I love that you put up with my stupid books.

And to Books by Adriana Locke (Facebook group), All Locked

Up (Goodreads group), and Addy's List (blogger group)—you make my dreams come true. I love you.

About the Author

Adriana Locke is a USA Today and Amazon Charts Bestselling author with a knack for writing swoony, unforgettable contemporary romances. At nineteen, she traded her small-town roots for big-city life, only to realize her heart beats for quiet mornings and cozy chaos. These days, she's living her happily-ever-after in Ohio with Mr. Locke—her high school sweetheart—four lively sons, and two hilariously hyper Jack Russell terriers.

When she's not penning love stories that will leave you laughing and sighing, Adriana is battling the epic quest of missing silverware, "gardening" (a.k.a. chatting with her plants), or leaving her grocery list on the counter as she heads to the store. Grab a cup of coffee, settle in, and let her books whisk you away to a world of heartwarming romance and irresistible heroes.

Join her reader group and talk all the bookish things by clicking here.

www.adrianalocke.com